DEAD AHEAD

DEAD AHEAD

A Jo Spence Mystery

JEN WRIGHT

CLOVER VALLEY PRESS, LLC
DULUTH, MINNESOTA

Clover Valley Press, LLC
6286 Homestead Rd.
Duluth, MN 55804-9621
USA

This is a work of fiction. Any resemblance between characters in this book
and actual persons, living or dead, is coincidental.

Cover design by Sally Rauschenfels
Cover images © iStockPhoto.com

Author photo by Kathy Heltzer

Printed in the United States of America on acid-free paper. Sustainable
Forestry Initiative® (SFI®) Certified Sourcing.

Library of Congress Control Number: 2011942865

ISBN-13: 978-0-9846570-0-1

Other books by Jen Wright
in the Jo Spence Mystery Series

Killer Storm
Big Noise

*I dedicate this book
to the baby dyke who came to one of my book
signings—in your softball uniform with your
mom. You plopped down in front of me, crossed
your legs, and asked me if I was going to read. I
hadn't planned to, but I did. For you.
I was impressed and touched by your
strength and confidence.*

*I also dedicate this book to all of the lesbians
and gay men who are coming to terms with their
sexuality. I hope your family and friends accept
and love you. If you are struggling, know that it
does get better. Supportive communities are out
there. Keep looking. May this book in some small
way make you feel connected and valuable.*

Chapter 1

IN THE DREAM, I WASN'T EVEN wearing a helmet. I could feel the wind. It felt like my partner Zoey running her fingers through my hair, only the touch was multiplied a thousand times. The early spring landscape flashed by as I cruised the north shore highway on my Honda Silverwing GL 500, heading southwest along the edge of Lake Superior.

Riding without a helmet was so unlike me. As a female in a predominantly male profession, I could be tough, but I wasn't reckless. Though aware of my helmet's absence, I didn't let it bother me. I raced through the air without a care in the world, beginning to understand why so many cyclists risked their lives to experience the freedom of riding unencumbered by a helmet.

It occurred to me that this freedom was something I might not want to give up. The speed and the low-throated drone of the bike spoke to me like a lover. I swung left onto the entrance ramp of the Blatnik Bridge spanning the bay between Superior, Wisconsin, and Duluth, Minnesota—my hometown.

I've always hated this bridge because it sits so freaking high over the water. It makes me feel like I'm suspended in midair. The gleaming structure appears like a maze of metal strips to me. Some brilliant mind calculated the steel beams to make sure they could support the weight and length of each bridge section, but to me, they're just pick-up sticks like the ones I got for Christmas in my seventh year.

Curiously, in the dream, I loved the bridge. I felt no fear as I gunned the throttle and accelerated upward into the sunlight. The bridge could take me even higher into the ride of my life. The engine screamed almost in protest as I increased my speed. I paid no attention.

To my left, the historic lift bridge was up, and a large ship had just passed

1

through into the bay. More big ships were docked at grain elevators, and a coast guard cutter was moored in front of the convention center. To my right, small fishing boats motored up from the bay into the St. Louis River. Ahead of me, a semi flashed its lights, possibly signaling police up ahead.

Cursing, I looked at my speedometer and slowed down to the speed limit of fifty miles per hour. Because of my job in the Probation Office, I had to be circumspect when it came to legal matters—even speed limits—but I was irked by the delay. I wanted to career on this edge of pleasure forever.

My Honda cruised across the smooth asphalt bridge. As I reached the middle of the span, I noticed orange cones. I swerved around one, and then the next, instinctively slowing down even more, but it was too late. As I brought the bike down to forty miles per hour, I realized that there was no longer any bridge under me.

I looked down for a split second to the bay waters of Lake Superior. Several yards of empty space separated me from the place where the bridge continued. Zoey's face flashed through my mind. This could be it if I didn't make it to the other side. My front tire was inching toward the pavement in slow motion, but the back of the bike was dropping. I clung to the handlebars, catching air in a bad way. As my motorcycle was about to hit the edge, I jerked awake, breathing heavily with sweat covering every inch of my body.

I glanceed over at Zoey, glad that I hadn't disturbed her. Consciously, I adjusted to the real world. Sometimes when I wake up in the night, I feel pulled back into my dreams, but I didn't want to go back to that one.

Zoey was still sound asleep, but I was wide awake and wanting to get up even though it was only 6 a.m. on a Saturday. Reluctant to move away from her warmth, I resisted the urge to touch the dark curls framing her thin, sculpted features. Zoey's eyelashes lay closed over her intense green eyes. I pictured her long frame, lean and naked under the blanket and curved in all the right places. I snuggled in just enough to take in her light musky scent before gently slipping out of bed.

Had I not had a busy morning planned, I would have coaxed Zoey awake and talked to her about my dream. It hadn't been that long since she'd moved in with me. I savored every second of living with her, especially waking up to see her beautiful face on the pillow beside me.

Forcing myself to look away, I dressed and put on my hiking shoes before heading off down the trail with my two dogs: Cocoa, a black lab, and Java, a lab-springer mix. The last of the snow had melted, and the woodland path behind my home had dried enough so that I didn't have to watch my step for mud puddles or wet leaves. I enjoyed the pale green undergrowth just emerging from the earth under my feet. The air had that fresh scent that can only be found in northern pine forests.

As I followed my bounding boys through our woods, my mind couldn't quite let go of the dream. If I told Zoey about it, she'd ask me a thousand questions, trying to make me analyze the heck out of it. As a psychologist who formerly had a private practice but now taught at the local university, Zoey would want me to try to identify the source of the foreboding in my subconscious mind. I laughed it off. Sometimes a dream is just a dream.

Maybe I *was* experiencing a little pre-season anxiety. I thought about how heedless I had been about the danger of the bridge. Many dreams are like that. Fears invade them. I've dreamed about arriving late to a meeting. Even arriving naked to a meeting. Often, we do the most unbelievable and uncharacteristic things in our sleep worlds.

Having to wait through long Minnesota winters made the advent of motorcycle season all the more exciting. I couldn't wait. And as I am always careful when cycling in real life, why worry? I shook off the bad dream and imagined the steps I would take to get my bike ready before turning the key in the ignition.

I'll re-install the battery, which I've had recharging in the basement. I'll add fresh gas, turn on the access line, and fire her up. Last season, she started without complications. I'd already changed the oil in the fall. I'd also flushed the coolant and changed the spark plugs. I tend to obsess about my bike's mechanics, but that's why she's in tip-top condition.

When Zoey and I began dating in late fall the year before, she had noticed the gleaming vintage bike in the garage. She couldn't believe that I owned a motorcycle built in 1981. For a thirty-year-old bike, the Honda sparkled. Its jet-black paint was in good shape, and the cycle had a fairing with a built-in stereo, storage compartments, and hard saddlebags. The engine looked bright and clean, and the chrome was rust-free. When I stopped for gas, I often got offers to purchase it on the spot. I would smile and tell the would-be buyers to check CraigsList or eBay.

Older model Silverwings are relatively easy to find, as they tend to last forever. Clubs, blogs, and entire gatherings are dedicated to the thousands still out on the highway. These motorcycles aren't relics to cherish, but road-worthy bikes meant to be used. Fairly lightweight, they are especially prized by women and new riders. I use mine for both transportation and stress relief. At the end of the workday, I hop on my bike, cruise up the scenic highway toward home and the tight-knit community we call the Valley, and leave all my worries behind. By the time I pull into the garage and greet my dogs, I can't even remember what had been bothering me during the day. I miss my rides during the winter months more than I'd care to admit.

As head of Juvenile Probation in Duluth, I regularly deal with criminal behavior, addiction, and other influences that can do lasting damage to young lives. And recently, partly because I believe so strongly in how effective it can be, I'd taken over the Adult Drug Court program. The extra responsibility was adding to my stress level. I really needed some bike time to help me relax.

As I neared the final curve of the trail, I picked up my pace and almost ran to finish the walk. I planned to grab a go-mug full of coffee before heading to the garage. I let the dogs into their fenced-in yard, took the steps into the house two at a time, and headed down to the basement to retrieve the battery. When I burst back up through the cellar door, I nearly ran into Zoey.

"Whoa," Zoey said as she placed a hand between us. "What's going on?"

I felt a little embarrassed by my enthusiasm. "Sorry, hon, I didn't think you were awake."

"What's the rush? What are you up to?" Zoey narrowed her eyes and gave me a suspicious look.

I sheepishly replied, "I'm firing up my bike."

"Your bike?"

"My motorcycle. The snow is finally gone."

"Oh, I get it." Her knowing smile was encouraging. "Want help?"

"Sure." I felt a surge of hope that Zoey not only would approve of my riding habit but would also be happy to ride along as a passenger. "Though I have to get a cup of coffee first."

"Okay, I'll meet you out there once I've changed."

The snow had melted, but the temperature in the Valley was still frigid, hovering around 40 degrees. I was pushing the motorcycle season a bit, so I moved the bike out into the sun to help warm it up while I worked. I had just sat down on the bike when Zoey emerged from the house. I waited until she moved next to me before pulling out the choke and turning the key. It took about two full seconds with the starter whining before the engine turned over. I flashed Zoey a big smile as the distinctive sound of a well-tuned Honda motor filled the air.

Zoey ran her hand along the bike's fairing and seat, and then onto my thigh.

"Where's your riding gear?"

"Riding gear?" I raised my voice above the sound of the motor, wondering if the caffeine had kicked in or if her hand on my leg was causing the flutter in my heart. Or maybe it was just the vibration of the Honda under my legs.

"You do have leather?"

"Sorry, sweet, this is it. I just throw on a jacket and rain pants if it's cold." Confused about how Zoey would know about riding gear, I also felt a pang of worry because I know that I'm no fashion horse. Zoey had been gently pushing me to think a little about my clothing choices. When we first met, I was blissfully comfortable wearing only khaki pants, Pendleton shirts, and sweaters in cool weather. Heck, I only wore one type and color of underwear. When my work clothes became worn, I just rotated them into my around-the-house wear. I loved the simplicity of it.

Even though I'd been trying to vary my clothing choices, I still didn't have much of a hairstyle. My semi-curly dark hair has always done whatever it wanted to do. I go to Cost Cutters when the mop gets too unruly, but it has never met a hair dryer, a curling iron, or styling gel.

In contrast, Zoey cultivates an actual wardrobe and earrings and things. Each morning, she does her hair and matches her accessories to her outfit. I guess you would describe her as "put together."

After Zoey moved in with me, and at her insistence, I had begun to wear some of her clothes—fashionable jeans and even some of her nicer sweaters when we went out together. I silently promised that if Zoey would ride with me, I would wear whatever gear she wanted me to wear, within reason.

"Want to go for a ride?" I asked.

"Totally. Can you really drive this thing?"

"I had a bike before I had a car." I leaned into the saddle like I'd been born there. "Go get some warm clothes on. Gloves, too. I have an extra helmet."

"Okay, but we're going to talk about getting some leathers." Zoey's eyes had a glint in them that I recognized from earlier adventures. I knew from experience that it would be worth my while to indulge my lover in whatever tickled her curiosity.

I fully warmed up the bike and pointed it toward the road at the end of the driveway, waiting for Zoey. I've owned many cycles in my life, and nearly all of them have been Hondas. I felt comfort in the distinctive sound of the machine as it warmed to a smooth hum.

Zoey bounded out of the front door. She had on one of my jackets, thick gloves, and a big grin. I handed her the extra helmet, and she put it on with ease. As soon as she sat down on the seat behind me, I said, "Tap me when you're ready." As I pulled out onto our road, she leaned into me and held on.

Chapter 2

ON MONDAY MORNING, I RODE to work along the scenic north shore of Lake Superior. Following the fifteen miles of beautiful, rocky shoreline, I couldn't imagine a more impressive commute, its vistas changing dramatically from one day to the next. The freshwater lake sometimes looked like an inland sea—with dark, crashing waves—and sometimes the surface rested smooth as glass. Boaters, kayakers, shore fishers, and tourists littered the shore and water.

I pulled into the parking lot and backed my bike into its spot. Usually I park alongside all of the Harleys and crotch rockets belonging to the men in the office, but they were absent today. We'd had a soft rain, and most of my colleagues had opted to take their cars, but not me. I just geared up to enjoy the elements. Stowing my outerwear in the trunk, I remembered riding with Zoey and found myself smiling as I entered the building for work. I was already looking forward to my return trip home.

It's not that I don't love my job. In fact, I'd say I love 90 percent of it. I just love riding more. Some people claim that I have a compulsive personality. Maybe that's why I can relate so well to my probation clients who end up in Drug Court. I kind of get the addiction thing. I'm a coffee addict, for sure. And I like to clean when I get stressed. My need for order is legendary. But riding my Honda Silverwing on the open road takes me where none of those other obsessions can. The speed awakens all of my senses until the world drops away and I am alive in the moment.

At 7:50 a.m., I entered the door to the Probation Office and saw that the lobby was nearly full of clients waiting to see their PO's. I said "Good morning" to the group as I entered, and one guy with a tattoo of a hand flipping the bird displayed prominently on his neck smiled back at me. I guessed that he was fresh out of prison, waiting to see his supervised release agent. I hadn't seen him in the waiting area before, and I pitied the PO who would try to help him find a job. Jeannie, working at the front desk, caught the interaction and grinned at me. I expected a quick-witted comment from her about his tattoo once we were out of earshot.

My heightened senses from the ride made the smell of unwashed humanity in the room almost overpowering. Jeannie buzzed me through the security doors, and I squiggled my index finger at her, giving her our sign for air freshener. She nodded in agreement and went back to her typing.

As I traversed the short hallway to my office, Cat hollered from her end of the corridor. "Hey, Jo, I have to talk to you when you have a minute."

"Okay, I'll just ditch my coat."

I sat in one of her visitors' chairs. "What's up?" I looked at Cat, enjoying her morning-person energy. Even first thing on a Monday morning, she seemed alert, bordering on hyper. Her medium-length brown bob was expertly styled, and she was dressed in her usual pressed slacks and sweater.

"I locked up one of Johnson's clients—Trevor James. I got a call from the DPD last night at home. He's on probation for felony terroristic threats and disorderly conduct, and he blew a .21 on the P.B.T. I told the officers to lodge him at the jail. I faxed them a hold this morning under your signature."

Cat (Catherine to her mother) is the only PO I ever allow to lodge clients without actually speaking to me on the phone. She usually does call me, though, when she lodges one of Johnson's clients. He has a temper tantrum when anyone puts one of his clients in jail.

"What did Johnson say?"

"I couldn't reach him. Lucky me." She rolled her eyes. "Don't worry; James has a no-drink clause on his Conditions of Probation. The cop that picked him up is the one who originally arrested him. Said he is a total asshole when he's drinking. In the original offense, he threatened to kill his girlfriend, and when the cops tried to arrest him, he put up an impressive fight. He's one of those guys who doesn't react to pepper spray. He went berserk on them. Last night, he went nuts outside of the Nosy Bar after they kicked him out. It takes a lot to get kicked out of the Nosy."

That was an understatement. "Let me know if Johnson gives you any trouble."

"Oh, I will. I logged everything." She held up the filing report. "What's his story, anyway? Why doesn't Johnson like to lock anyone up? It's unnatural." She shook her head. "What PO doesn't like to hold their people accountable?"

"What's your guess?" I had my theories but wasn't about to share them with Johnson's peer.

"Lazy is my best guess. Also doesn't like paperwork."

"That isn't so unnatural," I said, and Cat laughed.

"You have a point."

As I moved toward the hall, she called after me, "Hey, Jo, I have a proposition for you. Eric and I are getting a membership at Tech Fit. We're going to work out over the lunch hour. You should think about joining us."

"Isn't Eric a fanatic? Are you sure you want to do that?"

"He is kind of a freak, but it's starting to rub off on me. I could lose a few pounds."

"I'll think about it," I said uncertainly, thinking about how different their lives were compared to mine. Both of them were young, and they lived in town. Eric, known for his vanity, was obsessed with his diet and fitness routines. His mode of exercising inside a facility seemed artificial to me. My walking, hiking, snowshoeing, and skiing in the great outdoors gave me all the workouts I thought I needed.

Making my way into my own office, I brewed a single cup of dark roast, cleared my voice mail messages, and scanned my email. I only had two meetings scheduled for the morning, and the rest of my day was free for handling the inevitable crises that arose in the office. The adult felony unit supervisor was on vacation, so I expected a number of additional reports to review and sign as well as case consults to fit in around the meetings.

Taking a break from the computer screen, I settled back into my chair and sipped my coffee. Alana (a.k.a. Alli), one of the juvenile intensive PO's, popped her head into my office door.

"Got a minute?"

I pointed to one of the chairs. "What's up?"

"You're going to get a call from Brian Jones's dad."

I nodded, allowing her to go on.

"I gave him your number, in fact. I'm sorry, but the guy's a jerk. He threatened me last night. Of course, he was subtle enough that I can't press charges, but I got his drift."

I nodded again, waiting for the full story to come out. She hesitated, and that made me curious. "What's the rest of the story? This isn't the first irate parent you've dealt with."

She put her head down a bit. "I kind of lost it with him."

"Tell me the whole story. Start at the beginning." I tried to picture her losing it with a parent and couldn't. Though she was still young, Alli took inordinate pride in her professional image. She'd been a state trooper before transferring to the Probation Office because she wanted to be on the prevention side of things. After only two short years as a PO, she had a definite air of confidence and competence about her. I tried not to smile, thinking about how even the most professional among us are still human.

"Okay, we screened Brian for pre-trial release from Juvenile Detention yesterday. He was charged with felony theft. I met him and his mother up at JD, and everything looked good. He's young. This is his first charge. Mom was supportive, so I released him. He's really a likeable kid. Big for twelve, but likeable, you know?"

I nodded and sipped my coffee.

"So I stopped by the house yesterday at the end of my shift to make sure he'd made the transition home okay. That's where it got interesting. The dad was home. Curtis Jones. He didn't want to let me in the house, so I explained to him that if we couldn't have access to the house, Brian would go back to JD. He went on a rant about freedom in his own home, so I tried to explain it to him again. Then he started griping about law enforcement and abuse of power, and I went off on him about how good parents should support their kids, especially when they're in trouble. I reacted to the comment about law enforcement." She looked genuinely remorseful.

"Did you swear at him?"

"No."

"Disrespect him?"

"Not really."

"Then don't worry about it. I'm glad you referred him to me. It's my job to back you up. What about Brian? Did he go back up to JD?"

"No. The mom came to the door, and she brought Brian outside where I could talk to him. When I left, I made it clear they needed to grant us access to the house or Brian would have to go back up to JD. I pointed my finger at him."

"Don't sweat it. Sometimes the families get to me, too. Just take it in stride and make a commitment not to let him get under your skin. He's probably just scared."

"He's not scared. He's angry, and he's paranoid. He scared *me*. You should have seen the look in his eyes when I pointed at him; he wanted a piece of me."

I checked my voice mail messages and found nothing from Curtis Jones. Feeling hopeful that this would all blow over, I made a mental note to ask Lou, one of Alli's partners, about it later. He was scheduled for the afternoon shift in the intensive unit.

My two meetings took up the remainder of the morning, and I was glad to get out and walk with Jeannie down to the lift bridge at lunchtime. She commented about the client with the prison tattoo being someone's future son-in-law. After I returned from lunch, Cat popped into my office.

"We checked out the gym. It's awesome. Here's some info." She handed me a wad of flyers and papers. "It only costs $12 a month if you go eight times a month. Our insurance pays the rest."

"What? Am I getting fat?"

Cat laughed at me. "Just old. It'll be fun. Get your mind off of work for a while. It's a great stress reliever." Cat bounced as she talked. "Jon is totally stoked about me working out." She raised her eyebrows. "I'm sure Zoey would be impressed."

I felt my cheeks grow hot. "I'll think about it." Working out in a gym didn't sound that fun or exciting to me, but I loved that Cat wanted to include me in her plans.

The red light on my phone indicated voice mail, so I retrieved my messages. An angry male voice spoke to me in a controlled shout.

"This is Curtis Jones. Don't look me up in your system. I'm sure I'm in there. I know all about you people. You have no right to be in my house. I'm not on probation. He is—my son, Brian Jones. You can talk to him at the office. My number is 390-4598. I expect a call back."

I archived the call, brewed a cup of coffee, and dialed his number.

"Hello." The voice still registered just under a shout.

"This is Jo Spence, Probation Supervisor, returning your call."

"Okay. You need to know that you have no right to come into my house."

"Technically that's true. We can't enter without your permission, but we need your cooperation in order to supervise your son."

"You don't have it. You can meet him at your office. He's the one on probation, not me," he repeated.

"He isn't on probation yet. He's on pre-trial release. He hasn't entered a plea."

"There you go; using the court system to confuse the situation and violate citizens' rights. You have no right to come into my home."

I felt the hair rise up on my neck, and I resisted the urge to bang the phone down on my desk. "If we can't have free access to your house, you'll be responsible for sending your son back into detention. We'll have to schedule a detention review hearing. You can make your case to the judge."

He started to interrupt me, but I continued in an even tone. "I'll make a personal appearance at that hearing and tell the judge that you are refusing to grant us access to your house and that we can't adequately supervise Brian under those terms. In order for your son to remain out, we need to come in, search his room, and make sure that any weapons have been removed."

The man dialed up his volume. "I have a right to bear arms. You can't take my weapons. I know what happened in Waco. I know about the conspiracy. You're all murderers, and you're going to pay for it. You better watch your back." I pictured him spitting into his phone as he nearly screamed his hateful words.

"So, a hearing it is?" The phone slammed down in response.

As soon as I hung up the phone, I walked over to the intensive unit office where Alli and Lou were going through shift change.

"Hey, Jo, what's up?" Lou said without standing. I sat down across from him wearily.

"I just got off the phone with Curtis Jones. Guy's a little off."

Alli said, "I just briefed Lou on that. How'd it go?"

Lou is one of my most senior PO's. He loves field work enough to stand the late night and weekend shifts.

"We need to set up a detention review hearing for tomorrow. I want to be there. This guy is hiding something. I don't think he's just crazy." I had their attention. "Don't try to go into that house alone. Get police backup, or better yet, let's wait until after the hearing to pick Brian up. I don't want you getting hurt. Jones reacted when I told him we needed all the guns in the house removed."

"Okay, Jo, but why do you need to go to the hearing?" Lou asked. "We can handle it."

"Oh, I have no doubt you can handle it. I made this guy a promise I'd be there myself."

"He got to you?" Alli seemed surprised.

"No, but he scares me. This guy is dangerous." I didn't want to admit to them how much he *had* unsettled me.

Chapter 3

I HOPPED ON MY BIKE at the end of the day and noticed an occupied car at the back of the lot. The windows were darkened, but I could make out the outline of someone sitting behind the steering wheel. I sensed him watching me. My mind flashed on Curtis Jones for a moment. No, it was probably just someone waiting to pick up a spouse. I finished securing my helmet and took the alley toward Second Avenue West.

Duluth is a little like San Francisco when it comes to steep streets, with her mile-wide hillside facing a big body of water. As I turned to go down the hill, I noticed the car begin to come into my field of vision in the left side mirror. I couldn't quite make out the face, but I could see someone with short blond hair wearing a baseball cap and sunglasses. I abandoned my usual route, which takes me on a coaster-ride thrill route down some of Duluth's most vertical streets and instead took nearly level Second Street heading east. I made my way all the way to 21st Avenue before turning down the hill toward London Road, where a strip of gas stations, restaurants, and other commercial establishments had sprung up adjacent to the shoreline. The car, a dark older model Camry, followed three car lengths behind me.

When I got to the Holiday gas station, I pulled in to see if the car followed. It kept going straight. I filled my tank and proceeded home along scenic Highway 61, once I was sure I was free of my escort.

The temperature struggled up to 55 degrees, and the air felt crisp on my face. My helmet has a face shield, but I could feel the wind blowing in off the lake, and I could see white caps. Along the shore by Brighton Beach, the waves crashed into large dark rocks, sending plumes of spray well over six feet high. The big lake was in a playful mood.

As I pulled into my driveway, my dogs Java and Cocoa went crazy inside the fence. I smiled at their happy, high-spirited welcome. I knew they were looking forward to our evening walk even more than I was. As Zoey wasn't yet home, I ran inside and changed into my hiking boots. I opened the gate to our fenced-in yard, and the pups ran straight for the trail.

I consciously took two deep breaths, inhaling the fresh smell of wet earth and the hint of green budding trees, and then set off at a fast pace. The light rain that had fallen overnight had left the trails wet, but there was little standing water. As I hiked, I thought about the car that had followed me from work, and the veiled threat from Jones. Then I shook the thoughts off.

Zoey's car was in the garage when I finished my walk, so I quickly toweled off the dogs, left my wet boots in the entryway, and opened the inside door. Zoey called out from the bedroom.

"Hey, hon."

"Hi."

"I'll be out in a sec. I'm getting out of my work clothes."

Zoey came out of the bedroom in a pair of jeans and a black sweater.

"You can't wear that sweater and expect to keep it on for long," I said as she came toward me.

"That is precisely why I wear it." She gave me a flirtatious smile. Her mouth was smiling, but her eyes held a wistful expression. "You'll have to control yourself, though. We have a dinner invitation from Donna and Kathy."

"Right now?"

"As soon as we can get there—they're making lasagna." Zoey walked up to me and pulled me into an embrace. "Get out of those wet pants, and we'll head out."

"I thought you liked me in wet pants?"

Zoey smacked me on the butt and said, "Get."

During the entire three-mile drive to Kathy and Donna's, I was distracted by Zoey in that black sweater. She has a tall, lean, but slightly curvaceous figure, and she knows how to dress to highlight her assets.

Sometimes I wonder what she sees in me. I'm totally unaware of my physical presence, and I'm sure it shows. In my younger days, I got hit on a lot, but it wasn't my wardrobe that caught anyone's attention, and I know my physical attractiveness doesn't begin to compare to Zoey's. I looked down at my khaki pants that were identical to the ones I'd shed after the dog walk and vowed to work harder at looking better. For sure, I'd indulge Zoey in her quest for riding gear.

A herd of deer that had been feeding at Kathy and Donna's bird feeder scattered as we pulled up to the house. The charming single-story home sat built into a hill overlooking Lake Superior and bordering the Little Knife River. In winter, we would likely have snowshoed or skied there under moonlight or wearing headlamps. Spring brought ample daylight but difficult navigation where we cross the river. So we drove.

My best friend Kathy had built their entire house with the help of friends. One would expect an architect to construct a mansion, but Kathy preferred to design and build green. The modest home had large south-facing windows, a two-foot overhang on the north and south sides to shade the sun in summer, and a simple interior design with built-in cabinets and ample woodwork. She'd installed solar panels along the roof on the south side to heat their water supply.

Kathy's partner, Donna, worked with Zoey on research projects at the U, and they had become close friends. It was Donna who had first introduced me to Zoey.

When Kathy came out to greet us, she was wearing her signature duct-tape-patched overalls. She had obviously showered and cleaned up after her workday in the shop, but her clothing didn't reveal a speck of vanity. I felt our kinship and looked forward to a comfortable evening.

As we sat down to a dinner of vegetarian lasagna, garlic bread, and salad, we caught up on our days. Donna had dealt mostly with colds at the U Health Clinic. Kathy had been constructing prototype eco-friendly cabinets to be installed in the kitchens she was designing for a builder. Zoey's students were progressing well in her classes. I hesitated, not wanting to tell my friends about the threatening parent I had encountered during my day, so I tried to stay quiet and hoped no one would notice. My plan didn't work.

"What about you, Jo? You're so quiet over there," Kathy said.

The whole group turned to me. "I had a boring day. The usual things. You know—reviewing reports, signing warrants, doing case consultation. Mostly boring."

"What about the part that wasn't mostly?" Zoey squeezed my hand on the table. The look she gave me told me that she knew I was trying to hide something. I knew better than to keep up the charade.

"Well, I did receive a call from an irate parent."

"What happened?" Zoey asked.

"The parent wouldn't let us into his house to supervise his kid. The mom has been cooperative, but the dad is a nut case. He got a little scary when I told him he would have to remove his guns so we could supervise his son. He went on a rant about Waco and government conspiracies. He thinks all government workers are plotting against him. He should know that in government, it's a miracle if two departments even communicate."

No one smiled. Instead, eyebrows shot up all around the room.

"What else?" Zoey pushed. She knows me so well sometimes that it's eerie. I couldn't get away with anything around her.

"I'm not sure, but I think someone followed me partway home. It's probably just my imagination. You know, getting spooked by the guy."

"What else did he say?" Zoey kept digging.

"He said we needed to be held accountable for the Waco conspiracy. Something like that."

"So, he threatened you!" Zoey visibly stiffened.

"Jo, you have to think about getting another job," Kathy piped up.

"I love my job." This conversation was predictably going downhill fast.

"And it's going to get you killed. Maybe both of you." Kathy looked at Zoey. Kathy knew she had no leverage talking to me about this, but she just might find some if I thought Zoey could get hurt. "You should work with me. I'll teach you to run a CAD program. Or better yet, you could take up carpentry. You could specialize in building green kitchens or bathrooms. It would be great fun."

I actually smiled at that. There were times when I fantasized about producing a measurable, tangible product rather than persisting at my chosen profession. For some reason, I had made it my mission to guide youth away from re-offending, and now I was trying to help drug addicts get clean. When dealing with human weaknesses, the outcome is never certain, and some situations can prove to be dangerous. My friends had been pressuring me for the past two years about quitting. And in the short time we'd been together,

Zoey and I had already survived two near-deadly brushes with criminals.

"That's an interesting offer, my friend, and I'll give it some thought. Let's see how this thing goes. We're setting up a hearing tomorrow so this guy can have his day in court. I'm planning to give him his say without placing myself too prominently in the middle."

Chapter 4

WHEN WE GOT HOME that night, Zoey wanted to know if I was seriously thinking about changing jobs. I told her, "Not really," but the building idea was interesting to me. Kathy and I had built my house, and the project had been a labor of love. The satisfaction of standing back and admiring something I had produced was gratifying. The house turned out great, too. A post-and-beam-framed, single-story ranch home with a basement, its large windows overlooked a wooded ten-acre lot. It boasted a deck on the south side and a screened porch on the north. I thought it couldn't possibly be improved. That is, until Zoey moved in.

She warmed up the feel of the house with her elegant touches in décor, such as the sheer panel curtains she bought to grace the large window openings in the dining room. We had tried them out there first because I wasn't convinced that we needed curtains blocking our view of the outdoors. The results had been spectacular, and we were planning to purchase more for the living room.

As she sat next to me at the kitchen island, she said, "Do you feel like car pooling tomorrow?"

"Sure, hon. Do you want to drive or ride?"

"Let's take your bike."

"Really?"

"Really. I'd love to ride to work with you between my legs."

"I see. Are you sure you can work after that?"

"Not sure at all, but I'll try.

The ride in Tuesday morning was beautiful despite the cold. Spring days in Duluth start out around 35 or 40 degrees and warm up slowly until noon. Zoey didn't complain, though, and she even took her helmet into work with her. I rather liked picturing the look on her colleagues' and students' faces when they noticed the helmet in her office.

I arrived at the Probation Department at eight on the dot. The waiting area for clients was only sparsely populated. As I entered my office, I noticed a sticky note on my computer from Lou indicating that the Jones hearing was set for eleven in front of Judge Mason.

I smiled at that, since Mason is a seasoned judge with lots of juvenile experience and not likely to take any chances on a case with a nutty father. Sometimes it's a crapshoot with judges. When the usual juvenile judge isn't available, you could get some pretty unexpected rulings. That would not be the case here. Mason was solid.

After I signed my inbox of warrants, discharge reports, and various court orders, Dale, one of the adult intensive supervised release PO's, stepped into my office.

"We could use your help down here, Jo."

I jumped up and followed him to an interview room where a client appeared to be under the influence. Two PO's were standing by outside the office in case John needed backup as he interviewed the client.

"So, what prescriptions are you on?"

"Here, I brought 'em," the client said with slightly slurry speech.

"Says here you were prescribed sixty Clonipine the day before yesterday, and you're supposed to take one every six to eight hours. Where are the rest of them?"

"Don't know. I took some. The rest should be in there."

John poured the contents of the bottle out onto a clean piece of printer paper. "There are only twenty in here; forty missing."

John poured the contents of another pill bottle onto a separate piece of paper and put on a pair of latex gloves. "Where are the rest of these? You were prescribed twelve OxyContin, and now there are only six."

"I have a bad back. Need 'em for the pain."

"We're going to give you a UA today. What's it going to show?"

"These are prescription meds, man. They're all legal."

The client looked agitated and kept darting his eyes toward the backpack sitting next to him on the floor. He started to stand up, but Dale pushed him back down in his seat.

John reached down and took the backpack out of his reach. "We're going to search this for our safety."

"You're not going to fucking do anything. That's my property." The client looked behind him, saw several of us ready to intervene, and got more agitated.

"I'm going to jail, aren't I? Well, you think I'm going to jail? I could fucking kill all of you."

At that point, I left the area, retrieved a police radio from my office, and asked dispatch for assistance with an arrest and possible new charges.

"Probation to dispatch"

"Go ahead, Probation."

"We need assistance with an arrest of subject..." I turned to Dale. "What's his name?"

"Bruce Reynolds."

"Subject is Bruce Reynolds. He's intoxicated, agitated, and making threats."

"Squad 26 responding."

"Squad 24 responding. Squad 40 responding. ETA four minutes."

With several PO's standing by, we searched his pack. Inside, we found pornographic material, a large knife, and some free-floating pills on the bottom of the pack. All of the evidence was bagged and tagged and placed in the evidence safe in my office.

Six squads converged and took Bruce into custody without incident. As the last officer left, I followed him out. Squads covered every exit, and every available driving lane was blocked.

"Why such a big response?" I asked, once the client was secured.

"He's a regular. Always resists, sometimes with weapons."

"We found a knife in his pack."

"Where is it?"

"We kept it."

"Good. Nice work."

"Thanks for the help." I nodded my appreciation.

I updated the PO's in the office about why we received such an overwhelming response from the police, and they commented on how we regularly deal with unpredictable and dangerous clients every day and don't always have all of their background information. I reminded them that it's our job to prepare for the worst case scenario every time. I also gave everyone a pat on the back for handling a tough situation well.

Lou, Alli, and I walked over to the courthouse together for the eleven o'clock hearing in Mason's courtroom. The hallway outside was vacant. The light marble walls and floors echoed our every word.

"Looks like we have a no show," I said to Lou and Alli.

"I'll go check with the bailiff," Alli offered. When she poked her head back into the hallway, she said, "They're in the interview room with Randolf."

"The public pretender?"

Lou was being sarcastic, so I shot him a look. "Hey, without public defenders, none of this works," I said. He rolled his eyes.

We camped out in another interview room, waiting to see if Randolph wanted to speak to us before the hearing. After a few minutes, the bailiff came into our room.

"You're up."

Once we were inside the courtroom, Lou sat down next to the prosecutor, and when the judge gave him a nod, he stood and introduced us to the judge and for the benefit of everyone in the courtroom.

"Your honor, present today are Brian Jones, his parents Curtis and Ellen Jones, Public Defender Andrew Randolph, and I am Lou Ornado from the Probation Office. Also present from Probation are Alli Brown and Jo Spence. To my right, your honor, is Hal Martin from the County Attorney's office. We are here today to review detention."

"I see that the juvenile is out of detention. What's the issue?"

"Your honor, we screened Brian for intensive supervision while he was being held at Juvenile Detention. He was cooperative; his mother was supportive; so we released him. When we went to his house yesterday, his father refused to let us enter. He also made threats to our officers. We can't supervise Brian without full access to the household."

"Mr. Randolph."

"My client has done nothing wrong, your honor. In fact, it's my understanding that this has to do with Mr. Curtis's right to bear arms. Probation, specifically Ms. Spence, told Mr. Jones that he would have to turn over all of his guns."

Jones began to speak loudly. "The government has no right to enter my house and interfere…."

Randolph put a hand on him and whispered, "Let's let this play out."

"Ms. Spence?" The judge looked over his glasses at me.

"I spoke to Mr. Jones yesterday. He was aggressive and threatening toward our PO's, and me for that matter, when I explained our need to enter his house in order to supervise Brian. When I told him he would have to remove all guns from his property, he became belligerent. I'm not talking about taking his guns; I'm asking him to store them elsewhere…for the safety of everyone involved."

"Mr. Jones."

"The government has no right to remove my weapons. I did nothing wrong."

"Mr. Randolph, please take a moment to discuss this with Mr. Jones. Explain to him that this isn't about him. This is about trying to keep his son out of detention."

They stepped out of the courtroom briefly and then returned.

"Mr. Jones would like you to consider having Brian report to the Probation Office rather than utilizing traditional ISP. Your honor, while this is an unusual request, this is Brian's first offense. It is a property crime rather than a person crime, and it's not unheard of for clients to be released under their own recognizance under these terms."

"Where does the prosecution stand on this matter?"

"We request that he be supervised under the Intensive Supervision Program as previously arranged, and that the parents be ordered to fully cooperate with all of the terms and conditions of that program. To allow less supervision because a parent is uncooperative is setting a bad precedent."

The judge scratched his head and pondered things for a moment.

"I'm going to grant your request for office visits to the Probation Department, on a daily basis if necessary. I will tell you that any violations will result in detention, or increased supervision."

"Thank you, your honor," was murmured, and all parties moved out into the hallway.

"That's a hell of a thing to do to our office," Lou muttered. "This is going to be hard for us to pull off in intensive. Can you assign it to a Felony PO?" Lou asked.

"I'll take him on myself," I said. "I don't have any clients right now, and you know I like to keep my hand in."

Lou gave me a doubtful look but kept any disapproving thoughts to himself. "He's all yours."

I walked over to Brian. "Brian, I'm Jo Spence."

"Nice to meet you, ma'am."

"Please call me Jo. I'm not that old."

"Yes, ma'am. Err, I mean Jo."

"When are you done with school?"

"3:10."

"How long will it take you to get to my office?"

"I can be there by 3:30."

"See you at 3:30 tomorrow, then. Here's my card. Call me anytime. I'll probably stop in at your school sometimes to save you the trip."

Curtis glared at me as I spoke to his son, but I ignored him. Mrs. Jones was silent and looked sheepish as we parted ways.

Chapter 5

As soon as the hearing was over, we all walked silently back to our office. I couldn't tell if my PO's felt undermined, supported, or neutral about what had happened with Jones.

At lunchtime, Alli and Eric headed out the door with their gym bags. I tagged along. Alli flashed me a big smile. They jumped into their workouts on the cardio machines as soon as we arrived at the gym. I stopped at the front desk and asked for a tour. My guide was a mid-forties former bodybuilder named Annie who had maintained quite a physique by adding a workout here and there throughout her day.

"This facility isn't a meat market like some of the gyms in town," she remarked as she hustled me through the free-weights area. She had a lot of energy for someone her age. "We cater to people who are serious about their workouts, and we respect those who don't really want to socialize at the gym." She looked at me appraisingly.

I nodded and glanced around. The place was well-lit and clean.

We were about to move on when I noticed a tall blond woman doing squats with a staggering amount of weight. She was a knockout and strong. *Wow, she's built like a brick shithouse,* I thought. I must have stared longer than was polite because she slowly brought the bar to rest, rose to her full height, and walked over to us.

"New recruit?" she said to Annie.

I put my hand out. "Jo Spence."

She stared mutely at me for a moment, without offering me her hand, and then replied, "Interesting." Then she slowly walked away. I looked at Annie to try to figure out what had just happened.

"Don't take it personally. She's a bit eccentric. I assume she thought… well… she's gay… I'm gay… you're?" She looked at me expectantly.

"Gay."

"She seemed to recognize your name."

"I work in probation. We don't often win popularity contests. Perhaps I've dealt with someone she knows."

She nodded sympathetically and said, "Well, I wouldn't let it discourage you from signing up here. She usually keeps to herself, but she can be territorial. You won't use her favorite weight bench, will you?"

"Oh, no, no, no. I wouldn't think of doing that!"

Annie laughed. I liked her. She might be reason enough to come back to the gym.

I picked Zoey up at Campus Central after work. When I drove up on the cycle, she stood next to the statue of a scholar/athlete posed with her helmet. I totally cracked up. She held the pose long enough to see me laugh and then ran over to the bike.

"I love this motorcycle-pooling," she said as she fastened her helmet and slid in behind me. She tapped my shoulder as soon as she was ready, and we headed out. The temperature had climbed to 60 degrees, and the sun shone. I could see a large number of scooters as well as sport bikes in the parking area.

As soon as I pulled out onto College Street, I noticed the same dark Camry idling at the side of the road—the one that had tailed me, if it had been a tail. The car pulled out and followed us. I did a quick U-turn on College Street. The driver of the Camry also tried to do a U-turn but couldn't quite manage it in one shot. I quickly pulled into a side road and made several turns. I lost him.

Zoey tapped my shoulder and yelled, "What was that?"

"We were being followed." Zoey put her arms around me. "I lost him, but we're taking the back way home. I don't want to take any chances."

Zoey held on all the way home. When we got there, I started my routine to walk the dogs, but Zoey decided to join us. The trail was a tad drier, and the earth smell was slightly less pungent.

Zoey walked fast. "Was that the same car following us?"

"Yes."

"Who do you think it was?"

"I'm not really sure. It might have to do with that whacko parent I'm dealing with, but he got his way in court today. I really don't know. I'm sorry if I scared you with my driving."

"Your driving didn't scare me, but I knew something was up." Zoey shrugged.

"I liked your pose by the statue." I tried for a little normalcy.

"I am pretty funny, but the change of subject isn't quite going to work. What are you planning to do?"

"I'll call Nate tomorrow. Have him look into the parent's background." Nate is one of my best friends and colleagues at the Police Department. We started our career at about the same time roughly twenty years ago. We help each other out whenever possible.

"You get a lot of whacko parents?"

"I get all the whacko parents. That's part of my job. I talk to the ones who are unreasonable, drunk, or just out there somehow. The PO's have their hands full with the kids. They don't need to be dealing with all that, too."

"How many do you get? Whacko parents, I mean."

"Couple a month. None are this paranoid, though. They have high expectations for justice, for magic rehabilitation, or for getting restitution paid right away. I usually have to explain the real world of criminal justice to them, and then they back off."

"Your job must suck some days."

"Some days, but mostly it's pretty routine. I actually like the interesting stuff. It breaks up my day. I take it as a challenge."

We finished the walk, ate dinner, and lazed in front of the fire, with Zoey grading papers and me reading a book. Zoey said she still wanted to commute on the bike in the morning, adding, "I'd rather keep an eye on you."

As we slid into bed, she mentioned that we needed to do a little shopping after work the following night. "I'm getting quite the fantasy about you, me, and some leathers. We need to do some shopping." With Zoey's arm over my waist, I fell asleep wondering what her fantasy might involve.

Chapter 6

AFTER DROPPING ZOEY OFF at the university the next morning, I started my workday in my usual predictable manner. I made coffee, checked voice mail and email, and fielded questions from staff. Then at 9 a.m., a day that had been skimming along so smoothly developed a new wrinkle.

From the corner of my eye I noticed movement outside my window. The building across the street was a five-story red brick square, much like our own. A rather large, completely naked man was climbing down, or rather attempting to climb down, the outside of the building. He had a rope tied around his waist and a pair of tennis shoes on his feet, but that was the extent of his attire. I watched in fascination as his fat red cheeks inched down slowly while his legs jiggled from the strain of his effort.

I picked up my police radio, but I had to wait an eternity for radio traffic to clear.

"Probation to dispatch."

"Go ahead, Probation."

"Please send squads and an ambulance to Second Avenue West and Third Street. I'll call in the details." I knew better than to broadcast over the air what I was seeing, as it would draw a crowd.

That is precisely what this guy wants. I hated to think about what the bricks were doing to his front side as he inched his way down. I telephoned dispatch and relayed the scene, then walked down to Sharon's office. She's one of the probation officers who specialize in sex offenders. I looked out the window, pointed, and asked, "Is he one of yours?"

Her eyes got huge. "Not sure. I'll grab Sean and go take a look."

"I'll join you." When we got outside, we learned that the client was

31

indeed one of Sharon's. As we walked up, he looked at me expectantly.

"What's this about, Mack?" Sharon demanded. He refused to respond, but he had a smirk on his face and seemed to enjoy the attention. The police put a coat on him and led him to a squad. He kept looking back—at me. I felt an uneasy wrench in my gut.

"What do you want to do with him?" the officer asked Sharon.

"Are you charging him with anything?"

"Indecent exposure. It's only a misdemeanor. He'll be out by tonight."

"I'll draw up a warrant and hold him on a Violation of Probation. I need to figure out what's going on with him. Is he hurt?"

"Some scrapes. Nothing the nurses at the jail can't handle."

Through the open squad door, Mack still looked back at me eagerly.

"She's not impressed by this," Sharon said to him before shutting the door and looking away.

"Do you know him?" she asked me.

I shook my head no. This was starting out to be an interesting day. I wondered if I might regret my conversation with Zoey about enjoying the challenge of the unusual. No, this wasn't challenging, it was more like bizarre. I spent a chunk of the morning debriefing staff about the event, encouraging everyone to get back to business as usual.

At 3:30, I got a call from the front desk, "A Brian Jones to see you."

"I'll be right out."

I escorted Brian into my office, and we settled at my conference table.

"Nice office," he exclaimed. "How come your office is nicer than the others?"

"Observant, aren't you? Because I'm the boss."

"You aren't my PO?"

"I'm your PO."

"Because of my dad?"

"No, I just like to be a PO sometimes, too. I like kids. Why would you think I'd have you because of your dad?"

"'Cause he's crazy." He took his finger and made a circle by his temple.

"What do you mean?"

"He thinks everybody's out to get him. You know. He's always mad at the police, teachers, and the government. He's crazy."

"How is he with you?"

"He's okay. I mean, when he's not going off about his theories, he can be pretty cool."

"What do you need from me to help keep you out of trouble?" He laughed at that.

"What's so funny?"

"I never expected you to ask me questions. I guess I expected you to boss me around. You know, be hard on me."

"Well, my job is to help you figure out you. I can't make you do anything and have it last. Sure, I can lock you up, but unless you want to change your life, it's only a short-term fix. If you decide to change, it will last. Do you want to change anything about your life?"

He hung his head. "Lots of things."

"How about we start with just one. A small one so you can see how this whole thing works."

"I want to do better in school."

"Great. That's kind of a big one. Can you think of a smaller thing you'd like to change? We'll get to the school problem eventually."

"How about quitting pot?"

"Sure. That's a big one, too, but what the heck. How much do you smoke?"

"When I have it, or when my friends have it."

"Like once a week? Once a month?" I didn't want to lead him too much.

"Couple times a week."

"Why do you want to quit?"

"Wow, I expected you to go off on me, tell me it's against the law or something."

"I'm here to help you as much as you want to be helped. I can give you urine tests and bring you back to court if you want, but like I said, if you decide to do something on your own, we have a much better chance of long-term change. Lasting change. So what about smoking is making you want to quit?"

"It's not fun anymore. I just feel dead inside. Sometimes I start to get paranoid, and I remind myself of my dad. I really hate that."

"Those are great reasons to quit. Have you tried to quit before?"

"No. I just go along with everyone else."

"What do you think would happen if you said 'no, thanks' to your friends?"

"I don't know."

"Want to try it and see?" I gestured palms out, like it wasn't a big deal.

"Yeah, I'll try it."

"Need anything else from me today? Are you safe at home?"

He laughed. "I can see why you'd ask that, but I'm okay. Are we done?"

"See you tomorrow." I found myself looking forward to my daily talks with Brian. In only fifteen minutes, I'd learned a lot about him. I liked him right away.

When I picked Zoey up from work, she stood at the statue in yet another pose. It cracked me up again.

"To the leather shop, driver," she shouted as she walked toward me. Before she got on the bike, her expression changed to a serious one. "Tell me what the car looked like. The one that followed us."

"It's an older black Camry with darkened windows."

"I'll watch for it."

As we were pulling out of the Central Campus circle, Zoey and I spotted the car at the same time. It blocked our exit. "Fuck."

I handed Zoey my phone and told her to speed dial #2, which was Nate's direct number. She had to put it on speaker phone to hear anything. She began to describe what was happening.

I eased the bike up and over the curb and onto the sidewalk that ran between two buildings. I followed the sidewalk until I reached a parking lot. Crossing the lot, I exited out onto St. Marie Street.

The Camry was able to keep us within sight as it circled the block of buildings we had passed through. The car was gaining, but lagged about a block behind us. Zoey relayed our location to Nate as I kept making turns.

"I'm going to the Police Station," I yelled so that both of them could hear.

As the car slowly gained on us, we heard a shot. The window of a car parked next to us on the side of the road shattered. I gunned the throttle, making a beeline straight down the hill toward the cop shop.

I lost sight of the car. Slowing enough to take a turn into an alley that ran parallel to Lake Superior, I eased the bike into a driveway and pulled up beside a house, killing the engine. We both listened.

All I could hear was Nate continually saying, "Zoey, are you okay? Where are you?" I took my helmet off, Zoey handed me the phone, and I told Nate where we were. We both waited on the bike until he arrived.

"I think that was a woman," Zoey said.

I looked at her, surprised. "Are you sure you got a good look?"

"No. I just caught a glimpse. The jaw line. Seemed feminine to me." She pointed to her own. I shook my head. The possibility didn't seem likely.

"Maybe not, though. I was a bit distracted. Did you call Nate today to have that parent checked out?"

I grimaced. "Sorry, I forgot."

"You forgot. How could you forget that?" She sounded incredulous.

"I had an interesting day," I said weakly.

Nate drove up, squealing to a stop, followed by two squads. He lumbered up to us. "What have you gotten into now, Jo?" He stood with his hands on his hips.

"Thanks for coming."

A uniformed officer brought out his notebook and pencil, and interviewed us before calling in a description of the vehicle and directing another squad to examine the parked car with the shot-out window. When I started talking about Jones, he turned the interview back over to Nate.

Nate offered to escort us home, and we continued the interview at home over coffee.

"Why in hell didn't you call me earlier about this?" he stormed. Nate was angrier than I'd ever seen him.

Zoey remained silent and didn't even look at me. I stared at my cup.

"I'll check into Jones first thing tomorrow. We'll have so many men on him; he won't even be able to shit without us knowing about it.

"Jo, you have to bring me in on things before they blow up. You could have been killed."

"I really appreciate you helping now," I managed to say.

"It's probably a good thing you were on your motorcycle. I don't think you could have escaped in that Range Rover of yours. That really took some driving."

"I was scared shitless. It's amazing what you can do when someone is shooting at you."

"Want me to stay with you guys tonight?"

"No, I'll set the security alarm. I'm sure he doesn't know where to find us."

"See me first thing in the morning. We'll figure out a game plan about this guy."

Chapter 7

ZOEY AND I DIDN'T RIDE TOGETHER in the morning. I was glad, but it pissed me off at the same time. Some idiot was endangering us and interfering in our lives. I stopped at the office to put one of our senior PO's in charge, and then set off for the two-block walk over to the Police Department in City Hall.

The DPD takes up a significant portion of the City Building. The City, County, and Federal buildings were all built at the same time, forming a three-sided perimeter around a circular drive and a statue of Sir Duluth. They are well adorned with marble and granite. Even the floors and stairs are marble.

Nate sat in his tiny cubicle, with his big frame nearly filling the small space. Each time I enter the Police Department, I'm shocked at how shabby such a beautiful building can look. Stuffing the entire DPD into such a small area with 1980s fabric cubicles that only go halfway to the ceiling is probably the only way they could have ruined the space.

The makeshift cubicles stood in stark contrast to the formal marble walls and floors that embellish all the government buildings in the circle. I pondered what the economy must have been like for the community to be able to build such elaborate facilities. Perhaps it was during the mining boom.

I looked up at Nate, who was wearing his reading glasses—always an entertaining sight.

"Hey, Nate, got any coffee?"

"Let's go to a coffee shop to talk. You won't fit in here."

"Ground Under?" I asked hopefully.

"Perfect."

We took Nate's unmarked Crown Victoria. He admitted that it was good to see me alive this morning. Nate and I had been through a lot together, including apprehending a hired hit man after he tried to kill me at my house.

Once we had our lattés, he updated me on his research.

"From what I can tell, Jones is small time. He has a couple of arrests for disturbing the peace, and he was charged with making a terroristic threat against a teacher at his son's school. That's it. I pulled the report on the threat. When Brian's teacher suspended him, his dad went ballistic. Curtis Jones claimed she was part of some conspiracy, and he threatened bodily harm. She got a harassment order and transferred the kid to another teacher. End of story, as far as I know."

"Any stalking?"

"Not sure. I plan to interview her. Here's another interesting thing, though. He has two other kids. Both older than Brian. They've come up on the radar of the community liaison officer for stealing. We haven't caught them yet, but it's only a matter of time."

"So, other than interviewing the teacher, do you have any ideas?"

"I want to put Jones under surveillance. Push him. This guy will go off, and then we can arrest him. Get him off of your back. For sure, I want to see what kind of car he drives."

"I need to go with you." I looked him in the eyes.

"It'll be tonight, after you're done with work."

"Fine. I'll bring the pizza." I knew all of Nate's weaknesses.

"Make it meat lover's, and you have a deal."

My day at the office was low key. I emailed Zoey to tell her I had to work late. I told her I'd call her from the stakeout.

Brian showed up at 3:30, and to my surprise, he was eager to talk to me.

"Hi, Brian. How was your day?"

"Boring. School is boring. How was your day?"

"It's very nice of you to ask. I've had a good day."

"I made some progress on my smoking. Remember we talked about seeing if I could say no if my friends or brothers offered me some pot?" He looked at me to see how I'd react.

"I do remember. How did it go?"

"When they offered me a joint, I said, 'No, thanks.' They kind of looked at me funny, shrugged, and said, 'More for us.' That was it."

"How did your night go without it?"

"Fine. I kind of missed zoning out when I was home, you know. I couldn't tune out from my dad. Otherwise, it was fine. Just like any other night." He relaxed his slim frame down into his seat like he wanted to stay awhile. He wore baggy jeans that hung down below his hips and a loose-fitting T-shirt. His tennies were bright white.

"I'm proud of you." He actually blushed at that. "This is a first step, though. What do you think your next challenge will be?"

"If I get into it with my dad. Sometimes I need to smoke to tune him out. He's such a jerk sometimes. He won't let up. If I don't back down, I know we'll get into it."

"You mean it'll get physical?" He nodded, embarrassed. My guess was that he'd suffered many blows at the hands of his father.

"Have you ever been able to walk away from an argument?"

"Yeah, but mostly when I'm stoned. Then I don't care. I can chill."

"Is there something you can repeat in your own head that will help you not react to him? Like a saying you keep repeating."

"Like 'don't let him get to me'?"

"Would that work?"

"Probably not, but it's worth a try."

While I was talking with Brian, something niggled at my conscience. While I had taken on the role of probation officer with the lad, I was simultaneously helping to gather evidence against his father. Pursuing both tasks at the same time raised some ethical considerations for me but also might lead to conflicting loyalties on Brian's side of things.

"Brian, you know that your dad might face consequences for things he's done that aren't legal, don't you?" I chose my words carefully, trying to gauge Brian's emotions.

"Yeah, I guess so."

"With adults, the system can be a bit tougher because adults are expected to behave more responsibly. So, he could be looking at real jail time. How will that sit with you?"

"Even if he's locked up, it won't change the fact that he's my dad." When Brian turned to look up at me, I expected to see his usual expression, the nonchalant eyes of an adolescent. Instead, I saw an expression that showed he was older than his years. I've seen that look in the eyes of convicts doing twenty years to life and couldn't help wondering what damage his father had already caused.

Boys often try to emulate their fathers, even if those fathers are absent or emotionally distant. It seemed that Brian was aware of his dad's delusions, but he couldn't see a future without his controlling influence. What would happen when Brian was confronted with the difficult choice to either bond with me and follow a path away from crime or remain loyal to his father?

"If your dad gets into trouble with the law, remember that you still have your mom. And now you have me, too. Remember what I said. Call me anytime."

After Brian left my office, I sighed. Difficult choices. We all faced them. Brian would have to make his choice sooner or later, even if I didn't intervene to make his father face justice. No, I didn't feel sorry for going after Curtis Jones. It might make Brian's path clearer if he saw his father brought down.

Chapter 8

I MET NATE IN THE PD GARAGE at five o'clock, leaving my cycle in the Probation lot. We stopped to pick up pizza and pop before parking the undercover van on Jones's block. The van was a classic '70s converted Chevy with shag carpeting, a bed, and captain's chairs up front. The windows were all darkened. A two-way mirror was installed on the side panel so we could see out but no one could see in. We munched pizza, watched the house, and got genuinely bored. There was no sign of Jones or of the Camry.

After dinner, three boys left the house together on foot. We waited an hour, and one by one they returned, each on a bike. They brought the bikes into a garage behind the house and then went right back out, returning later with three more bikes. We snapped pictures, and in between runs, I went to the convenience store to pee, picking us up some not-so-fresh coffee.

"I can't believe you drink this stuff. Aren't you the legendary coffee snob?" Nate complained.

"Oh, *contraire*, my friend, drinking this makes the good stuff all the better."

I called Zoey to give her an update.

"You should see this van. It's totally ugly. Shag carpet. Eight-track stereo. We have to get one."

"Anything on the car?" Zoey was not amused by the van.

"Nothing. It does look like our little darlings are running a stolen bike ring. Haven't tied it to dad, though. The night is still young."

"What time will you be home?"

"When the kids stop bringing bikes in."

"I'll wait up. Call me before you leave, please."

"Okay."

Darkness descended, but the streetlights kept the area well lit. Mr. Jones came out to the garage. This time when the kids came back, they were carrying a big bag. Nate called in for silent backup and tensed up as he waited.

"You will not leave this van. Clear?"

"Clear, boss."

As soon as backup squads arrived, I watched Nate join the other officers and silently converge on the garage with guns drawn. Nate listened at the window before using his radio to signal something. The officers waited until the garage door opened. Once the three boys and their father moved outside, the police surrounded them, shouting, "Freeze, police!"

All four suspects were quickly handcuffed. As he interviewed Curtis Jones, Nate leaned down into his face. Suddenly, Jones head-butted him.

The other officers were all tied up with the juveniles, so I jumped out of the car, ran to Jones, and pulled both of his arms up and away from his body, causing him to yelp. Nate's nose was bloody, and he looked at Jones like he wanted blood of his own.

"You just bought yourself an assault charge, buddy. Jo, help me put him in the squad."

We tucked him into one of the waiting squads before I had a chance to see about Nate. His nose was still bleeding, and he was going to have two black eyes. That would only draw attention to how tiny and close together his eyes are relative to his monstrous size.

"What did you say to him?"

"Nice, blame the victim," he said with a grimace. "I asked him about a black Camry. He started talking trash about you, so I leaned in to make my perspective clear to him, then bam, he head-butted me."

"What was the trash talk?"

"He referred to your sexuality. He thinks your girlfriend's pose by the statue was pretty funny."

"Really" was all I could say, but my gut dropped, and I must have looked a little pale. I glanced over to see the officers taking the teenagers into custody. Brian studiously avoided looking back at me.

"Don't worry, we'll charge him with resisting arrest, assault, contributing to the delinquency of minors, and anything else we can think of. I'm showing this pretty face to the judge and prosecutor at arraignment to influence his bail. Let's go into the garage and look for a Camry."

We didn't find one, but there were piles of stolen items in the garage, including car stereos, bikes, and small electronics. Nate had a hunch that they had been selling the stuff on eBay. He said he'd look into it right after the court hearing.

Nate dropped me back at the office. It was clear as we pulled in that my cycle had been tipped over. I jumped out of the van before it had come to a complete stop. Nate helped me right my Honda in spite of his sore nose. The only real damage was a broken turn signal. The engine guards and foot pegs had absorbed most of the impact.

"I want his ass in jail," I said quietly. Jones was crossing a line that really pissed me off. A thirty-year-old bike isn't always easy to find parts for, let alone ones with matching paint.

Nate pointed to his nose. "Trust me, Jo, he will be."

I called Zoey with an ETA before heading home. I took my time driving in the dark. My headlights picked up two deer grazing on the early spring grass beside the roadway. I didn't want to incur any more damage that night.

Chapter 9

I HAD TROUBLE GOING to sleep. Once I finally drifted off, I dreamed that Zoey and I were riding on the bike together. Her arms were around me, the sun warmed my face, and we were driving up the north shore along the lake. I leaned into a curve right before a bridge.

Suddenly the engine died, leaving me barely enough momentum to bring the bike over to the side of the road. Then a semi came around the curve toward us. The massive truck came over the line, and there was nothing I could do except wait to see if it hit us. The driver locked up his brakes, and I startled awake.

"Bad dream?" Zoey mumbled.

"Bad motorcycle dream."

"Want me to listen?"

"No, go back to sleep. I'm getting up for awhile."

"Ice cream?

"Ice cream."

"Tell me about it first." She touched my arm.

I told her about the dream.

"Are you afraid of riding after being chased?"

"No, the bike saved us, remember?"

"So, it's the chasers that have you worried."

I nodded yes, and she let me go.

I padded into the kitchen and dished up a bowl of chocolate ice cream. I set the bowl on top of the woodstove as I added logs. Before long, we wouldn't be lighting a fire in the evenings. I'd have to use the microwave to melt my ice cream just the way I liked it.

I let the ice cream soften while I pondered my life. That offer from Kathy looked pretty good at the moment. Whenever Zoey and I came close to getting into a fight, it always involved my job. I wondered if it was worth it.

I ate my ice cream and went up to bed, but I was still too restless to sleep. Finally, I took pity on Zoey and settled in on the couch. I managed to snooze for an hour before Zoey, Kathy, and Donna woke me.

"What the heck? Some kind of party I didn't know about?" I muttered.

"No, we're ganging up on you." Kathy had an expression on her face that told me to just go along with them.

"We think you should quit your job. Here's some coffee, by the way," Zoey said.

They all huddled in a tight circle and leaned in toward me. With no way to escape, I made a conscious effort to relax, uncross my arms, and listen.

Each one took her turn, trying to convince me to leave my job. Kathy started out by saying, "Come work with me. I promise I won't stalk you or threaten to kill you."

Donna added her two cents' worth by saying that I needed to think about my long-term health risks due to living with so much stress all the time. Zoey added that I was having too many bad dreams and not getting enough sleep. She also said I needed to think about the impact my job was having on her and on us.

I listened quietly, sipped my coffee, and replied, "I'm thinking about it."

They all had shocked looks on their faces, expecting me to put up a fight, and then they walked into the kitchen to scrounge up breakfast. I could hear them murmuring amongst themselves, and then I looked up to see Zoey watching me from the doorway to the kitchen.

"I'm proud of you."

"What for?"

"For not getting defensive. It would have been easy for you to do that."

"I don't think I have the energy. It's not like what you guys said to me hasn't crossed my mind." She came over and rubbed my neck and shoulders.

I felt grateful for the support, and for not feeling like we were at odds over this, but in a way, their "intervention" had only compounded my stress.

Chapter 10

THE NEXT DAY STARTED WITH yet another Mack encounter. As I entered my building, I noticed a man sitting just inside the entryway on the floor. I assumed it was a drunk sleeping off his binge drinking episode of the previous night.

Once upon him, I recognized the beefy grin of Mack, the guy who had shimmied down the neighboring brick building. He popped right up in front of me in a couple of ways. He was wearing the obligatory rain slicker. Flashers must consider them their professional uniforms.

I spun him around, put him in a bent-arm hold, and marched him up the stairs and into the Probation Department. The door buzzed, and I pushed him through the security door and right into Sharon's office, hollering to the nearest adult probation officer, "Bring your cuffs."

I leaned Mack face first into the wall and waited for the arresting officers to arrive. He started to complain about his arm, so I wrenched it a good one, causing him to go completely quiet. At least he wasn't stupid. I didn't waste another word on him.

Once he was cuffed and seated, I left him in Sharon's care, telling her to see me when the dust settled.

My next stop was the bathroom, where I washed my hands thoroughly before going into my own office to brew up a pot of coffee. I still had a slimy feeling, so I used a double pump of alcohol-based handwash. By the time I was able to take my first drink of coffee, Sharon and a couple of adult PO's were escorting Mack out of the building in handcuffs and shackles.

It wasn't long before Sharon hurried back in with a contrite smile on her face.

"So, what happened to the warrant?" I couldn't resist asking.

"Well, it got entered into the system all right, but the jailor who was processing his release didn't do a double-check on the computer for holds filed since he was brought in. I'm guessing the jailor will be docked a day of pay for that one." She folded her hands.

"Did you ask him if he was targeting me?"

She smiled at the question. "Do you really want the answer to that?"

I nodded yes, not at all amused.

"Well, Jo, it appears you made a big impression on him the other day when he was arrested. He wanted to know your name. In fact, he thinks you're his soulmate, and he doesn't understand why you didn't appreciate the warm welcome he gave you this morning."

I scowled.

"He thought maybe you just had a bad morning and didn't really intend to be mean to him."

"He hasn't seen mean," I said, gritting my teeth. "Please tell me that he's locked up for good. What do we have him in for?"

"Indecent exposure and fifth degree sexual misconduct. I'm not sure about how long he'll be locked up. The guy's nuttier than a fruitcake. I've been trying to get him civilly committed, but they keep saying he's more of a criminal. You know the runaround. He keeps missing his rule 20 evaluation to determine competency. I keep trying to hold him in jail until it gets done. Vicious circle."

"Does he know who I am?"

"He knows you're Jo, and that you're one of the supervisors. That's it."

"Let's keep it that way."

Chapter 11

NATE CALLED AT TEN and asked if he could bring Lou into the Jones investigation. He wanted to meet at Ground Under to share what he had learned so far. Lou wasn't scheduled until noon, but I called his cell, and he agreed to come in early.

Ground Under was its usual bustle. Mostly inhabited by college students, the coffee shop's quiet music mixed in with boisterous chatter. We sat in the corner at a table and worked to hear each other.

Nate had two black eyes and tape over his nose.

"Poor baby," I said without thinking.

"Hurts like a son of a bitch." Nate didn't seem to want to linger on it. "Here's what I have on Jones. We think he's part of a skinhead group."

"What?" I set down my mug.

"You got it."

"Don't they shave their heads?"

"Not necessarily. Not if they want to blend in. He's a serious racist—part of a group of over twenty. We did some Internet searching and found he's been selling the stolen merchandise on eBay. We have the stuff from his garage in our evidence room, so it'll be easy to track stolen items on his sales list. He's toast."

"Pure white toast," Lou said. I had momentarily forgotten about Lou's mixed race. Maybe it was a reason not to bring him into this. With his tall good looks, part Hispanic and part Native American, he could charm almost anyone, but skinheads?

"Why do you want Lou involved? He can't blend in with that group." Nate gave me a shocked look. Lou laughed.

"His experience in gangs might really help us. We need to figure out how to infiltrate this group. I know Lou can't do it himself, but he can help us figure out how. We need to identify all of them first. Lou has experience in making gang I.D. books. Can you reassign Lou to us for a few days while we figure this out?" Even though his eyes were bruised black and blue, he managed to look as eager as a puppy begging for a treat.

I looked over at Lou, who nodded enthusiastically.

"It's safe?" I asked.

"He's only consulting."

I chewed on it a bit. *He's my most valuable staff in the unit. Yeah, we could manage without him for a few days, but I want him safe. Lou wouldn't be armed. I guess I can't protect him forever. Once he retires in a few short years, he'll probably be hired by the PD as much as they can get him.*

The biggest hang-up really was that I would miss him. He was more like a peer to me than any of my staff. I had learned to count on him.

They both stared at me as I considered the assignment. "Okay, you can have him for awhile if you keep me in the loop."

"Excellent," Nate said.

"Thanks, boss." Lou's dark eyes brightened.

"Jones has his arraignment hearing today. He'll be a late runner in front of Mason. I plan on showing up with this in full view." Nate pointed to his nose. "I'm hoping to influence bail. Jo, can you come and talk about how Jones stalked you and took a shot at you?"

"Do we know for sure it was him?" I asked. I really hadn't gotten a good look at the driver of the Camry.

"Who else?"

I had to agree that it was probably him, but then again, how many of our clients were completely happy checking in with their probation officers? We were often blamed for their incarceration, especially on repeat offenses. We were the ones supervising their lives when they finally got out of jail.

Before court, I ran to the Honda shop to buy a blinker. Luckily, the store had one in stock. I took out my tools and installed it right there. It felt good to put some order back into my life. This would all be over soon.

The courtroom was filled with what we presumed to be skinheads or their sympathizers. Lou studied the crowd, wishing he could snap some pictures, but his memory would have to do. A jailer escorted Jones, dressed in a jail-issue blue jumpsuit, into the room. That meant he had been classified high risk and wasn't being allowed out in the general population at the jail.

I stepped into the hallway and used my cell to make a call. "Gerri, I'm at the Jones arraignment hearing. Why is he in blue?"

"Oh, he's a piece of work. He almost got himself killed by threatening every minority inmate he came across. We put him in segregation, and then moved him away from everyone in seg. He ended up strapped down in our intake room."

"You probably did him a favor."

As I walked back in, the bailiff spoke up. "All rise. Court is now in session. The honorable Richard T. Mason presiding."

Mason motioned for everyone to sit. "My docket shows this is a late arraignment. I have the paperwork. Mr. Strom?"

"Your honor, Mr. Jones has filed for a public defender, and he does qualify. I request that you appoint one for him."

"Public defender appointed. Please continue."

"We plead not guilty, your honor, and request a contested omnibus hearing and release on his own recognizance. My client is a long-time resident with a family and other ties to the community. He has kept previous court hearings, and we'll have significant legal arguments at the omnibus hearing."

"Mr. Peterson, what's the prosecution's position on release?"

I raised my arm for the judge's attention. "Can I take a moment, your honor, to bring prosecution up to speed on a couple of things?"

"Make it quick, please."

I updated the prosecutor on recent events. The attorneys deal with dozens of cases a day, and I didn't want to risk this one missing something. I would have almost preferred that prosecution wasn't here. Then the judge would look to Probation for information. Once I gave him an earful, Peterson proceeded.

"We argue for high bail, your honor. The evidence against Mr. Jones is significant. He resisted arrest, causing injury to the arresting officer." He pointed toward Nate.

"He's made several threats to members of the Probation Office, including Supervisor Jo Spence." He pointed to me. "Those threats also included either following Ms. Spence in a high-speed chase involving gunshots that could have killed her, or contracting for said crime. Mr. Jones is classified as high risk owing to threats he made to other inmates at the jail. It is believed he is part of a racially biased group. In fact, prior to his transport for court, he had to be shackled and chained to the floor in a padded cell. His conduct at the jail proves that he poses a threat to himself and others due to his racist beliefs and remarks. We request bail in the amount of $500,000."

I did a silent cheer. Sometimes getting support from prosecutors is chancy. He had nailed it.

The courtroom filled with a low rumble of conversation. Judge Mason slammed his gavel down. "Not guilty pleas are entered. Set the matter on for a contested omnibus hearing," He paused and looked at the scheduling clerk. "April 22. 1:30. Bail is set in the amount of $300,000."

My team met outside briefly and agreed to regroup at my office following court. I brewed up a pot of coffee and broke out the chocolate.

"Three hundred thousand bail is good," Nate said.

"Five hundred would have been even better. Pretty hard to get on an indigent client," I added, trying to cut Mason some slack.

"Indigent, my ass," Nate's face turned red. He grimaced when his angry expression caused his nose to hurt. "Well, at least we won't have to worry about him getting out until this thing is over. You should be safe for awhile, Jo."

"You still need Lou?"

"Yeah, I want to infiltrate the group. I have just the officer in mind. Lou, did you recognize anyone from the courtroom?"

"There were a couple of parents of former intensive clients. They all live in the same neighborhood in west Duluth, close to Jones. What do you say we take a swing by the houses tonight and see what we come up with?"

"Sounds like a plan. I'm going home to rest." Nate pointed to his nose.

My day wasn't even close to being done. We had our Drug Court pre-court conference at 2:30, so I went back up to the fourth floor to Judge Silven's courtroom. She had championed the idea of a Drug Court in the area, and our office obtained the grant. I was the designated coordinator of the program because I had worked with adult DWI offenders in the past.

It was probably the single most challenging thing I had done in my career to that point. Drug Court functions as a multi-disciplinary team involving the judge, prosecutor, public defender, probation officer, police, treatment provider, chemical dependency assessor, and in some cases, a representative from the minority community to which the client belongs. The program works to keep nonviolent drug offenders out of prison and give them treatment and intensive probation.

The offenders go through treatment, then appear in front of the judge and the multi-disciplinary team—weekly at first. They participate in cognitive thinking groups, aftercare, and other counseling as necessary.

The reason coordinating Drug Court had been so challenging was that all of the team members had to learn a common language in order to work well together. The language included both legal and chemical dependency terminology. Then we had to agree on entrance criteria and when and how to dole out consequences for relapses. Understandably, the police and treatment folks tended to disagree on the best course of action for a client, and coordinating the process could be fraught with passion and turmoil.

We had been up and running for several months now and were starting to see some benefits in terms of how the clients were doing. Long-term addicts were beginning to look like the human beings we knew they were. It was a highly emotional program, but one well worth the effort.

I entered the courtroom ready to give it my best.

Chapter 12

I FINISHED OUT THE DAY, took my time on my ride along the scenic highway, and walked the dogs as soon as I got home. It felt great to have my routines back. Zoey wasn't home yet by the time I finished my walk, so I put some music on and got started on dinner. I put together a spinach quiche and fresh peas.

Zoey walked in with a big smile on her face. "Mmm, smells good." She walked up to me and gave me a hug.

"Good day?" she asked.

"Great day. Jones is in jail with high bail. We should be safe now."

"Great day, indeed." She kissed me and pushed me up against the sink. When we came up for air, I suggested that maybe dinner could wait. She replied by leading me into the bedroom. Our clothes were off by the time we hit the bed.

Even though Zoey and I had been living together for several months, I needed her like I needed air. Sure, we had a sweet and sometimes serene home life, but when we kissed, it tapped into some primal need I had to connect with her. When we made love, I could leave work behind. Nothing entered my mind except her. She knew intuitively how to respond to my body, how to read and control my emotions. All of the walls that I needed to maintain objectivity at work came tumbling down as she moved with me.

"Oh, my god," I cried out.

She murmured, "I prefer to be called Zoey."

"Oh, my god," I cried out again.

As we moved together, our bodies formed a union, and the warmth inside me spread. I felt totally open and vulnerable. Through heavily lidded eyes, I looked into her as I knew she would be looking right into me. Her eyes told me that she craved more.

With another hill to crest, I questioned my ability to move. Once I got to that place of total vulnerability, it was hard for me to do anything but hold on. It felt so good. I focused my attention completely on her, and then we lay there in a still place for what seemed like an eternity.

I thought about how lucky we were to have each other. We had this incredible connection. It scared me sometimes. *Could I possibly live my life and be this open to the world?* My breathing became ragged.

Zoey looked into my eyes. "Tell me."

"I can't face the world like this."

"You don't have to, hon, only here with me."

"This is changing me, though. Each time we go here, I stay a little more open. I don't know if I can do it."

"That means you're ready. It means you're safe to feel. You'll protect yourself when you need to."

We slid our hands out from inside each other, and I showed Zoey that my hands were shaking. "It scares me."

"Our love sometimes scares me, too." Zoey nuzzled her head into my neck. "Your walls are movable, not permanent fixtures in your life. You'll put them up and take them down as you need to."

"Really?"

"Really, but right now I'm ravenous." Zoey always wanted to eat after sex.

"Still?" I asked.

She laughed, grabbed my shirt off of the floor, put it on, and barefooted it out into the kitchen. I grabbed her shirt and followed. My legs felt shaky. We settled down in front of the fire, and I put a blanket over us both.

After dinner, my cell phone rang. I didn't recognize the voice at first because it was a woman I had dated ten years before. Diane Anderson.

"Hey, Diane. Yes, I remember you, of course." While we hadn't dated in ten years, she would pop up from time to time in my life and kind of creep me out. I got the sense that she was still holding out hope that we would get together again. I didn't think we'd ever really been together in the first place.

"I'm an Assistant Deputy at the Sheriff's Department now, and I wanted to call you right away with this. I heard you were having a really hard time with Jones."

"That's an understatement."

"Well, he bailed out. He also made some serious threats against you. He's one hateful guy, and he doesn't like lesbians. Since you've meant a lot to me, I had to call you."

I felt a little defensive. While I was grateful for the heads up, she seemed a tad too possessive in her statement. I shivered inwardly. *I barely remember dating her. It really wasn't all that memorable.*

"Thanks, Diane. I really appreciate the call."

"Let's do lunch sometime. I could use an ally in the field, you know."

"Sounds great. Thanks again."

I must have had a dumbstruck look on my face.

"What?" Zoey asked.

"Jones made bail. I have to call Lou and Nate. They're out there tonight." I dialed Nate's cell.

"He what?"

"He made bail."

"Holy shit! He must have resources we don't know about."

"A woman I used to know works at the Sheriff's Department. She called to tell me that he's making it well known that he can't stand lesbians. Even white ones."

"Can you stay someplace else, Jo?"

"Not that again! I can't keep moving in with Kathy and Donna." When I was single, I had taken refuge with my friends to avoid a hit man associated with a new gang in Duluth.

"Just temporarily."

"I'll think of something else."

"Wherever you go, make sure you're not followed."

In spite of my resistance, Zoey wouldn't agree to staying anyplace other than Kathy and Donna's. We showed up there with an overnight bag.

As soon as we walked in, my defenses came up. "Please don't lecture me about my job."

"No such luck, sweetie, I can't agree to that." Kathy was secure enough in our friendship that she told me what she thought, regardless of what I wanted to hear. "Quit tomorrow, take a couple of months off, then we'll go into green building full force."

They all worked on me ruthlessly as we ate pie and then played hearts. At 8:30, we heard a car drive up. I tensed.

I looked out the window and was comforted by the sight of a Sheriff's cruiser. When I saw that it was Diane Anderson approaching the door, I opened it and invited her in.

I was a little taken aback by how much she looked like Zoey. Same build. Similar hair. Of course, Zoey was about a hundred times more attractive to me. I made a mental note to go back through the list of women I had dated to see if there were similar physical characteristics.

After I introduced her to my friends and Zoey, Diane gave me her cell number and asked that I call with even the slightest issue.

I walked her back out to her car.

"Thanks again."

"No problem. I'm working all night and am pretty much going to camp out between your house and here."

"Wow, that's some protection. Thanks."

"I volunteered."

I watched her taillights fade down the long driveway. When I came back in, Donna was in my face.

"Who the heck was that?"

"She thinks she's an ex. More like we dated a couple of times."

"She's still hot for you. Does she even try to hide it?" Donna asked.

Zoey looked uncomfortable, but she didn't speak.

"She's just a peer wanting an ally. I don't have the energy to deal with her right now."

Zoey put her hand on my shoulder.

"You okay?"

"Not really. I'm not worried about Diane. She's a little creepy, but what can she do? The Jones thing scares me, though. He's a skinhead. He's got a whole group of associates at his disposal. Diane might be trying to help, but she could easily lead one of them here. I don't want to do that to all of you."

"You're not doing it, Jo. They are. It's this crazy job of yours."

I shot them all a look that said, *Back off.* "Look, I can't just up and leave my job right now. You guys care about me, and I appreciate that…really. But I have to see this through. I'm completely committed to our new Drug Court. I don't think you realize what you would be asking me to leave behind. I mean, it's a whole new way of thinking about justice. We're taking addicts out of jail and helping them. The whole system works together. It's totally out of the box, and it changes lives. We UA the living shit out of them. And we team it. Treatment, mental health, prosecution, judges. This isn't just a job for me. We help people. It's my career." Zoey blinked twice and backed up a bit.

"I think we need to get out of here." I turned to Zoey. "Tomorrow's Saturday. I'll take Monday off, and we can get out of town for a long weekend. Can you take Monday off?"

"My job really isn't like that, Jo. I have classes to teach."

"I'm going, then. I'll either draw this threat away, or escape it."

"I'll ask Ellen to cover. She owes me." Zoey gave me that look of hers that said, *Oh, no, you're not. You're not going to take this on alone.*

"All right, then, let's do it." I was sure we could leave this thing in the dust.

Chapter 13

I CALLED TO CHECK IN with Nate. "How'd it go?"

"They had a meeting of the minds last night at the Jones house. There were roughly sixty people there. We took down license plate numbers, and Lou is starting a gang book. It looks to us like they're planning something big."

"Do you have any idea how they got the bail together? That would mean finding collateral for three hundred thousand. In that neighborhood, his house couldn't be worth that much. How did they come up with it?"

"I called the jail last night. He posted cash."

"Really?"

"Our little theft ring has to be dealing in more than bicycles. We're trying to track individuals...see how they make their money."

"Keep me posted."

"Will do. Where are you going?"

"Ely. We're taking the bike."

"You'll have your cell phone?"

"Yup."

Zoey and I left the dogs at Kathy and Donna's, and headed up Highway 2 north of Two Harbors. The trees were budding, and the grass was greening up along the roadside. We got out to stretch our legs at the picnic area near the top of Highway 2.

The stand of white pines at the rest stop is roughly two hundred years old, and we couldn't help but be humbled in its midst. Zoey and I stood in awe at the base of a huge tree as the forest radiated a cool pine scent.

We lunched on sandwiches, and I took a moment to study Zoey before we headed on. Her remarkable beauty and inner strength made my emotions well up inside. I looked her in the eyes, held her hand, and said; "I really appreciate you, hon." She smiled in response. We had needed to connect. Zoey rode with her arms around my middle for the rest of the trip.

My mind flooded with memories of camping trips as we pulled into Ely, gateway to the Boundary Waters Canoe Area (BWCA). There is something about entering a town after being in the wilderness for days or weeks that endears it to you. The place bustled with busy outfitters, outdoor clothing stores, art stores, and cars loaded with canoes heading into the Boundary Waters. I already felt more relaxed when we pulled up to a B & B on the main strip.

The sign on the road said "Vacancy," so Zoey and I rented a room for two nights. It was a Victorian with old world charm and creaky floors. Our room was simple but large, with a private bath. The owner didn't bat an eyelash about renting to two women, and we figured out later that neither did his partner.

As soon as we unpacked, I checked in with Zoey. "Okay, love, what's on your agenda?"

"Is there a leather store here? I've been planning to take you shopping. Remember my fantasy?"

I laughed. "Okay. Leather store it is. I'm sure our hosts will know exactly what we're talking about. We could also just window shop and then ask at some of the stores."

"I'm for that."

"Let's take in the Wolf Center and the Dorothy Molter Museum while we're at it."

"We have all weekend." She smiled big. Zoey's eyes sparkled. I loved to see her happy.

It was a beautiful afternoon, sunny and windless. The town smelled of coffee, baked goods, and home cooking. We walked along Main Street, wandering into all of the outdoorsy clothing and camping gear shops. Finally, we made our way to the biker leather store.

Zoey got a kick out of making me model chaps and vests in front of the clerk. I dutifully obliged, and we left with a matching set. As soon as we stepped out onto the sidewalk, I noticed a Sheriff's cruiser down the block. I waved, and the cruiser moved on.

"That can't be Diane?"

"Looked like her."

"Would the Sheriff's Department send someone up here?"

"Not likely. Let me call Nate to see if he knows anything." I made the call, updated him on our trip, listened to how the investigation was going, and then asked him about Diane.

Turning back to Zoey, I said, "He's checking."

We made our way back to our lodgings, and I spied the cruiser again, this time parked down the block from our B & B.

Once we were back at our room, Nate called me back.

"You know this chick?"

"By chick, you mean Diane?"

"Yeah, yeah, Diane. How do you know her?"

"I dated her a long time ago. We didn't gel. Why?"

"She's not assigned to guard you, just volunteering on her own time."

"Shit," eased out of my mouth.

"What? Is she bothering you?"

"I don't know. It just seems like overkill."

"Want me to call the Sheriff and pull her off?"

"No. I'll pretend she isn't here." I closed the cell phone.

Zoey looked at me questioningly.

"She's volunteering on her own time."

Zoey scrunched up her nose in distaste.

"It's kind of like having my own personal bodyguard," I said, trying for humor.

"That's not funny," Zoey said. Diane had effectively dampened the mood for our fantasy, and Zoey was icy.

"Let's go to dinner. The Mocha Moose has fantastic food," I said.

"Fine. Maybe we should invite Diane." Zoey turned and started walking away from me, heading for the door. This was uncharacteristic of her, and I knew I needed to tread gently.

"Hon, what's up?" I touched her arm, and she stopped.

She turned a bit red, realizing how she had sounded. "Wow. Did I just say that?" She took a deep breath and went on. "Okay, here's the thing. I think you are clueless about Diane. Clearly, she's still in love with you. She doesn't even try to hide it. But, I think there's more going on. I think she's unbalanced. You can't see it?" She watched me closely.

"I just can't imagine it. We dated a couple of times. It wasn't all that memorable. I'm sure she just wants a friend in Corrections." I paused. "It can be lonely to be the only lesbian—the only gay person period. Not many gay men go into law enforcement."

"She's in love with you." Zoey shook her head.

We dropped the topic over dinner and shrugged off our disagreement. The Moose specialized in vegetarian fare, and I tried the warm mushroom spinach salad, and Zoey had a black bean burger with a bowl of homemade wild rice soup. We split their chef's special Mocha Moose torte for dessert with decaf. It was heavenly.

As soon as we exited the restaurant, I caught sight of a black Camry, with tinted windows, on the opposite end of the block from Diane's cruiser. I pulled Zoey to me.

"Can we leave this for later?"

"Don't be obvious, but isn't that the car that followed us?"

"No way," Zoey whispered, her attitude shifting abruptly.

"Let's go back to the B & B. Could you let the manager know what's happening? I'm going to find the back door, call Diane, and see if she can summon local help to go after him."

As I made my way out the back door, I called Diane's cell.

"Hey, Diane. Jo here."

"What's up?"

"Can you see that black Camry at the other end of the block? I'd like you to call for backup to go after him. That's the guy who's been following me."

"I'm on it." She disconnected.

I could see her cruiser driving up to the Camry. I quickly redialed. She didn't answer. I moved closer, careful to stay in the alley and out of sight.

She pulled in behind the Camry, blasted the siren once, and instructed the driver to step out of the car with his hands raised. Nothing happened.

She instructed him again to get out of the car. Then she approached the driver's side door.

I hit the call button again on my cell. She didn't even flinch in response.

I watched her say something into her radio. Then two shots rang out.

As soon as she went down, the car peeled out.

I ran over to her. I could see a bullet hole through her shirt but no blood. I felt for the wound and discovered she was wearing a bulletproof vest.

"So much for waiting for backup."

"Nice. I try to help, and this is the thanks I get?" she said through clenched teeth.

Zoey and the B & B owners ran up to us.

I grabbed Diane's police radio. "Dispatch, this is Jo Spence."

"Go ahead, Spence."

"Officer down, Third and Main, Ely. Please send an ambulance." I didn't wait for a response but turned my attention back to Diane. She looked like her chest hurt. Zoey and I waited with her until the ambulance arrived, then rode to the hospital on the cycle.

I called Nate while we sat in the waiting room. He retrieved the record of the plate Diane had run. It came back as a stolen car with stolen plates. The car was from Florida, and the plates were probably taken from a junkyard. They didn't match.

"I didn't see him that closely, Nate, but it wasn't Jones."

"What did he look like?"

"I didn't see."

"Nothing?"

"Same blond hair under a baseball cap. Tall. That's all I got."

"I'm guessing he'll dump the car. Steal something new. The Sheriff's Department is on it. Ely PD, too. They're a little miffed that your friend went in without backup."

"They aren't the only ones. I saw the whole thing. It was stupid, and she's not my friend."

"How's she doing?" Nate inquired.

"I don't know. What kind of injury can you get from being hit wearing a bulletproof vest?"

"One hell of a bruise. It can even kill you if the hit is over the heart."

"It was more in the middle of her chest."

"She'll hurt like hell but will probably be okay. You coming back?"

"I'm not sure at this point. We need to make sure Diane's all right. Then I'll talk it over with Zoey."

"Well, call me either way. I'll come up there to escort you."

"My hero."

"I'm serious."

"My serious hero."

Chapter 14

WE DECIDED TO STAY in Ely until Diane was out of the woods. An officer stood outside Diane's room, and another was assigned to cover our B&B when we were there. I was impressed with the local police support.

Diane had taken some huge risks. Zoey and I mulled over what exactly made her do it.

"What do you think is going on with Diane?" I asked, wanting Zoey's perspective.

"Are you referring to her going in without backup or being irrationally attached to you?"

"All of it?"

"She's in love with you."

"We didn't even date that long, and it was a long time ago. I'm not buying that. I've dated other women. They didn't do shit like this."

"You said she has tried to reinitiate things a number of times over the years, right? I don't know what her history is, but if she's experienced previous abandonment, and then you rejected her, it was likely a trigger to that abandonment. She may also have screwed up values. A lot of stalkers do. They think that they can literally own other people, and once they become fixated on an individual, they can't let them go."

"Can someone like that be treated?"

"Absolutely. The person usually has to realize it's a problem first, though."

"I'm guessing she has abandonment issues. Her parents divorced when she was young. Her mom tried to raise her alone but wasn't very functional after the divorce. What treatment would you suggest for that?"

"I'd walk through the abandonment with her. Help her see it through adult eyes. She needs to understand that her parents were screwed up, and her abandonment was about them, not about her being unlovable."

"Sounds pretty simple."

"It is, unless you're the one trying to work through it. Most people have repressed many of their feelings of loss and hurt, and then they manifest in weird kinds of behavior. In fact, it's not unusual for people to take great risks like we've seen here." She nodded toward the operating room door. "To diminish the power it has over you, you have to face it head on. Feel all of the loss. That takes a great deal of courage and strength."

"You are an awesome therapist, you know."

Zoey smiled at me. "I love that you think that, but I'm only one human trying to help. I lose patience sometimes. That's why I went into teaching."

We sat in the waiting room for another hour before I waylaid a nurse, "Can we get an update on Diane Anderson?"

"Are you family?"

"No, but I'm a probation officer. She's a colleague."

"Diane is trying to leave against medical advice. She should be fine, though. She has a large contusion. It's not over her heart, but it will certainly be painful. She's also at some risk for a blood clot. I'm afraid only family can see her right now. Can I tell her you were in?"

"Tell her Jo and Zoey were here."

We rode back to our B&B with a police escort. We both lay down on the bed in silence for several minutes, trying to absorb what had happened.

"Fuck."

"Fuck is right. You know, you have a way with words." Zoey turned toward me. "Do you think we're safe here?"

I shook my head. "Hell if I know. Let's call Nate and Lou and see if they've learned anything new."

Lou picked up after the second ring. "Is Nate there yet?"

"Nate? What are you talking about?"

"Didn't you check your voice mail? He should be there any minute."

"Why?"

"He's coming up to be your big manly hero. I applied for the job, but you won't let me carry a gun."

"You're still my hero, Lou. Do you know anything more about the skinhead group?"

"Yeah, tons more, but I'd spoil all of Nate's fun if I told you everything. He'll be there soon. Would you tell me something, though?"

"Depends. What's on your mind?"

"What's with this Assistant Deputy not waiting for backup? Tell me what happened there."

"I don't know. I saw the Camry and called her on her cell. She said, 'I'll take care of it,' or 'I'm on it,' something like that, and then she went off half-cocked. I tried to tell her to wait for help, but she hung up. The guy surprised her with the gun. Got off a couple of shots and fled. Did they find the car?"

"Yeah, at a used car lot. Now it looks like he's driving a Ford F-150. Tan single cab. All the cops in the Ely area have the description."

"You think he's still around?"

"I wouldn't be. I mean, the guy shot at a cop. He must know they'll be gunning for him. You never know, though. People do stupid things."

"Do they think it's only one guy?"

"Well, so far that's all you've seen, right?"

"I've only seen the one guy, but Jones is part of a group."

"Yeah, with resources. I'd be very careful, Jo. I've been researching skinheads. They're essentially a gang fueled by power and hate. There are a lot more of them in this country than anyone knows about."

Nate arrived at the B & B a little after 11 p.m. with fresh coffee and rolls. He immediately filled us in on the skinhead group. It took me a minute to focus on what he was saying because I was staring at his black eyes and swollen nose. The bruising had turned a deep purple, and he looked horrible.

He and his crew believed that the gang had ties to an elaborate national organization. That same organization had provided the cash for Jones's release. Nate didn't believe our guy was any kind of top leader—just one of their loyal and outspoken members. After he ended the update, I initiated a line of questioning of my own.

"So, while we appreciate you telling us all of this, why are you here? I mean, you could have done this over the phone."

Nate had a smudge of frosting from one of the donuts on his mouth, and Zoey pointed with her napkin to her own chin, helpfully letting him know when he had cleaned it off. His small swollen eyes peered out at us from his big head.

"It was the only way I could keep Lou working on the skinhead gang info. He was coming up here if I didn't."

"My big manly hero?"

"Precisely."

"Did you get a room?"

"Right next door, and the big four-poster bed is calling to me right now."

"Is there still a guard outside?"

"Yup. He knows I'm here, and he has my cell number. Get some sleep."

Zoey and I talked a bit about the continuing danger, and we were both feeling tense. We had so wanted to connect on this trip and play at being tourists. That clearly wasn't going to happen. I didn't sleep well, and when I finally did drift off, I had a disturbing dream.

Zoey and I were on the motorcycle. We were using an in-helmet communication system and were talking about the scenery when suddenly an angry male voice broke in. The voice told me to drive off the road. It kept finding new ways to tell me to kill myself. I was afraid to ask Zoey if she heard the voice, because what if it was only in my own head? Then she tapped me.

"What the hell is this?"

"You hear it, too?"

"Yes, I hear it. Is this some kind of open circuit? Pull over." She spoke loudly to compete with the voice. We pulled over and took off our helmets, but the voice continued. Zoey and I looked at each other with dread. "Do you still hear it?"

Zoey placed both hands on her ears and lowered her head in anguish. I would have given anything to stop the voice from terrorizing her. Even if I had to listen to the angry voice all by myself.

"Shut up," I said, looking around for the origin of the voice. "Leave her alone!"

I awoke to Zoey gently shaking me. "Jo, it's a dream. Wake up." She gently touched me. "Wanna tell me about it?"

"No, but we're not getting in-helmet communication." She gave me a puzzled look, and I got out of bed and got dressed.

"Where are you going?"

"Downstairs."

"Want company?"

"No, sleep if you can." I glanced at the clock. It was nearly 5 a.m.

When I entered the common living area, I felt the warmth coming from the fireplace. As I came around the corner, I spotted Nate's big boots crossed out in front of him as he sat on a chair facing the front door.

"Couldn't sleep?"

"Not in my room. I caught a few cat naps down here, though." He stretched. His five o'clock shadow was well into a grizzly, stubby mass. His brown hair and sideburns were turning grey, along with his facial hair.

As I sat down beside him, his cell phone rang. He emitted a couple of "Uh-huhs," and then said, "Okay, we'll be on the alert."

After disconnecting, he shared what he had learned. "They found a stolen truck not far from here. They don't know what he stole next. The guy stuck around. Now we don't know what we're looking for."

"Great." I paced.

"Let's go." Nate was serious.

I nodded in agreement.

"Leave the bike and ride with me. I can have a Deputy ride it back later."

"No way!" I blurted. "It's gotten us this far. It's much more agile than a car, and I can drive it in tight spaces where cars can't go."

"It would be better if you were driving something faster. With a passenger, you'd be hard pressed to outrun a car on the freeway."

I shook my head, "No, we're riding back the way we came." I didn't even know why I was insisting on it, but being bullied by an unseen stalker was beginning to make me angry.

"Sometimes I forget how stubborn you are." Nate gestured to his gun. "And you don't have this."

"Yeah, but we have you. If you keep close, we'll be all right."

I went upstairs and snuggled in with Zoey, easing her awake. She insisted on the two of us wearing our new leather pants and vests. We grabbed coffee and a roll from the kitchen and hit the road, with Nate tailing us close behind in his black Crown Victoria.

Every car that approached or passed made me nervous. I could feel Zoey holding on a little tighter, too. After a few minutes, I felt comfortable enough to reach for my go-cup of coffee that was cooling in the handlebar-mounted coffee holder. I sipped carefully. I didn't want to risk spilling any drops that might shoot back and hit Zoey. With all of the sugar I'd consumed in sweet rolls in the past twelve hours, I felt a little jittery.

When we got to the area of white pines, I saw a silver Mazda approaching in my rearview mirror, coming around a curve behind Nate. As soon as we hit a straightaway, the car bolted around both of us. It must have been a souped-up model, because it was fast. The windows were tinted, and I couldn't see inside.

As soon as the driver passed both of us, he tucked back into my lane and abruptly slowed. I nearly rear-ended him, which would have forced Nate to rear-end us. Struggling to maintain our balance as my brakes squealed, I moved over to the shoulder and stopped. Nate immediately turned on his roof lights. When the car didn't pull over, he gave two quick bursts of siren. The car sped away. Nate decided to slow rather than give chase, keeping his promise to stay close to us.

"What was that all about?" I said when we caught up to him.

"Hell if I know. I radioed ahead and requested help from the Sheriff who works Lake County. I wouldn't be surprised if it wasn't our guy taking another run at you."

I shook my head in disbelief. I felt worn down by the incessant chasing. I also felt amazed that I was still alive. *If the object was to kill me, why hadn't they succeeded? Were they just trying to keep tabs on me?*

"I think we have to search your bike for a tracking device. Then we'll figure out where to put you."

Nate got out of his car, and we got off the bike. We searched it for anything that looked out of place. On my third time around the bike, I opened the leather pouch on the fairing where I store my gloves and a spare set of sunglasses. On the bottom, I spotted a small black rectangular object. I lifted it out and handed it to Nate, who put on his reading glasses before exclaiming, "Yup. This is a tracking device. High end, too."

"Shit." I fumed.

"No, this is good. I'm going to put it in my car, and after I drop you somewhere safe, I'm going to lure these wise guys into a trap."

"With backup, of course."

"As much as I can get."

Nate pulled over in Two Harbors, so that we could safely go on to our destination, which was again going to be Kathy and Donna's. Before turning off, he asked me to stay available by cell and offered me his backup weapon, which I refused.

When we got to K&D's, Kathy came out of the house to meet us with the dogs. We made coffee, and I updated her on why our trip had ended so quickly. She refrained from commenting.

It took forever for Nate to call back.

"The little fucker got away."

"How?"

"I drove to Brighton Beach and waited with a six-pack of squads. When the Mazda drove up, we blocked the exits. He rammed right through the cars."

"Did you get a look at him?"

"No, the windows were too dark."

"So, what's next?" I didn't know if I should go home, stay at K&D's, or try to make another run for it out of town.

"We're putting you up in a hotel with an armed guard."

"What kind of hotel?"

"Super 8 by the mall."

"No, thanks."

"My house, then?"

"Let me talk to Zoey and get back to you."

I took a minute to think things through before approaching Zoey. She watched me, giving me a little bit of space. When I felt ready to talk to her about it, I nodded for us to go outside. I didn't want Kathy overhearing and weighing in on this conversation.

"That was Nate. The guy who tried to get us to rear-end him got away."

"Are we safe?"

"He's one soldier in an army of these hate-mongers."

"What are we gonna do?"

"Nate said the PD offered to put us up in the Super 8 by the mall with a guard."

Zoey grimaced. "I like the guard part."

"He also offered to put us up at his house. I'm not really down for that. We can't bring this madness into his home."

"Can we stay here? And be reasonably safe?" She gestured toward the house.

"Shit. I don't know. I don't want to put Kathy and Donna in danger. I think we should go home, arm the security system, and hunker down. We have the dogs to warn us. I'm tired of running."

"What about my work?"

"We have another day to see how things go before we make that decision. I could always go somewhere so you wouldn't be a target."

Zoey shook her head no and held me. "We'll get through this. We always do."

Kathy didn't put up too much of a fight when we told her we were leaving, and that never happens. She said she would stop over to see us later with Donna so we could all decompress and play a game of cards.

I said I would rather they didn't. Kathy took that solemnly. She was beginning to understand the seriousness of the situation, and she wasn't pleased.

However, our evening passed without incident. Lou called to see how we were doing. Before bed, Nate called and updated me on Diane, saying that she had left the hospital, and after her briefing on the status of the Jones gang, she was told to go home and rest. No one had heard from her since.

I relaxed a little. As heartless as it sounds, I was hoping that she might be too injured to "help" anymore.

Nate had said that Diane couldn't remember what the driver looked like. That didn't make any sense to me. She had to have seen him up close. My nerves tightened again as I realized that she might well know who that driver was and was planning to try something on her own.

Nate warned me that Zoey and I shouldn't be in the house alone. He felt we were in clear danger. When Zoey heard me arguing with him about it, she motioned for the phone. I put it on speaker mode and gave it to her.

"You're staying with us," she said, as uncompromising as I had ever heard her.

"It's a longer commute. More chance for problems."

"I'm a great cook," she responded. Now she had him.

"What are your specialties?" I pictured him shooting his eyebrows up and turning his head. It felt weird to know his mannerisms so well.

"You name it. Steak on the grill, a slow-cooked pot roast, shrimp and pasta, home cooked hot dishes. Heck, I'd even break out the wok if you wanted."

"Where would I sleep?"

"The basement has a guest room and a bathroom."

"And your security system is working, right?"

Zoey nodded vigorously and said, "Working perfectly."

"I better get going," Nate said. "I'll be needing to make a grocery stop."

Chapter 15

ZOEY ROSE EARLY on Monday morning to make caramel rolls, scrambled eggs, bacon, and coffee. Nate came into the kitchen and gave her a look of blissful adoration. His black eyes were starting to heal. They looked yellow and less swollen.

"Don't you think it's kind of strange that nothing has happened?" I asked Nate. The idea of staying in the house all day waiting for someone to make another move made me feel claustrophobic. "Maybe they've moved on."

"Let's hope so," Zoey said.

"I'm going to do a perimeter check before coming to any conclusions." Nate remained skeptical.

He put on a baseball cap, a light jacket, and hiking boots, and set out to look around the property. After about five minutes, my cell rang.

"Can you come out here and look at this?"

"Out where?"

"Out back. Behind your clothesline in the woods."

"Be right out."

Nate was twenty-five feet deep into my wooded back property. I found him bent over, looking at a tripod. Hanging off of the tripod was a bag of dog treats and a set of high-powered binoculars in a weatherproof case. On top of the tripod was a screw-mount where a camera or a camcorder could be attached.

"What the hell?" I fumed.

"Well, I guess this is why it's been quiet."

I looked at the back of my house from where we stood and could see my living room.

"Do you think they were taking pictures?" I couldn't fathom any scenario where the pictures would be of use to anyone.

"Let's leave this for now. Maybe we can set a trap to see who's been camping out here. I'll do a web search to see if pictures are posted anywhere."

"No fucking way!" I hadn't even thought of that.

Nate borrowed my computer to Google my name. Nothing came up that wasn't work related.

"Try 'Jo Spence, lesbian.'" Zoey suggested. I was impressed that she could think like a white supremacist.

"Try 'Jo Spence, lesbian extraordinaire.'" I always tend to joke when I'm nervous.

"Nothing came up. Maybe they're using the pictures internally for something." Nate looked concerned.

"Any way you look at this, it isn't good." My voice sounded strained. Zoey reached over and massaged my neck muscles.

I tried to relax and enjoy the rub, but my mind kept focusing on a voyeur in my backyard. I remembered that Zoey and I had made love in the living room, in front of the fireplace. The thought of a video of us possibly out there somewhere made me angry and afraid at the same time. Zoey felt my tension increasing, stopped her massaging, and put her arms around me.

"What, babe?"

"I'm thinking that, depending on how long that camera has been set up, they may have a video of us making love."

"I'm sure the lights were low." She tried to reassure me.

"Let's hope so." I felt violated on a very basic level.

Nate came up with a plan to find out who had been watching and either photographing or videotaping the house. Using sewing thread, we set up a trip line in a 50-yard perimeter around the tripod. The trip line was attached to a radio frequency transponder that would indicate a perimeter breach. Once the thread was tripped, it would have to be restrung manually. Because the woods were so densely forested, we couldn't cover a very large area, but the lines might at least give us an indication when someone was out there. This was Nate's tried and true way of tracking intruders.

I had my doubts about his plan. There was a high probability that deer or other critters would trigger the warning system. However, I was grateful for every bit of protection we could muster.

A squad was assigned to monitor my road for anyone who might park there to walk in. Having done everything possible to secure our position against would-be stalkers, we were free to go back to our normal routines, as long as we stayed put.

I yearned to take my motorcycle and hit the open road, to free my mind and try to make sense of our situation, but that was out of the question. Nate was staying, and Zoey was cooking, so I had nothing to do but look forward to one more evening at home.

While Zoey worked on her grading and instruction preparation, I went out to my shop. I had to do something productive to feel in control again. Carpentry might do the trick.

I had bought an Adirondack rocking chair to use as a pattern, planning to make a matching one for our porch. Before I could begin work, I had to start with a shop that was clean and organized. I turned on the radio, swept the floor, and put away the few stray tools that littered the workbenches.

Nate wandered in and asked if he could help. I set him up tracing patterns onto the wood pieces, once I ripped them and cut them to length. I even showed him how to cut out the legs on the band saw. Once he finished cutting the pieces, I put a slight rounded edge on them with a router. Then I sanded them smooth. After an hour of work, we had all the pieces for one chair ready for assembly.

"This isn't so hard," he declared.

"It's pretty rewarding, too. When you're done, you can sit back and say, 'Hey, I made something.'"

"I think I still like the feeling of locking up a criminal better," he said.

He had a point there.

"Right up to the time when they get released," he said.

"Spoilsport." We smiled, understanding each other all too well.

We took a coffee break with Zoey before assembling the chair. Once we were done, we both stood back and admired it.

"That's pretty cool. It only took us a couple of hours." Nate's face shone with pride.

"It's yours. Try it out."

He scrunched up his nose. "No, I'm only a volunteer here, and a student."

"I want to give it to you. I'm so grateful for everything you've done for us. You know, staying here. It's definitely over and above."

"Not necessary."

As I opened my mouth to protest, he interrupted, "…but damned considerate." He sat down in the chair and began to rock. "I love it."

"And when you find a girlfriend, we'll make you a second one."

He maintained strict control of his features and wouldn't respond. I tried harder: "Or a boyfriend." This made him laugh out loud.

On our way back into the house, his cell phone rang. I gave him some privacy while he fielded the call, and went in to deal with the laundry from our aborted weekend trip. I love hanging clothes out on the line in the spring, and I amused myself by pinning up a pair of Nate's boxers. *Let the videotapers get a load of these.*

When I came back into the house, Nate was waiting for me.

"What's up?" I asked.

"The shit's hitting the fan in town, and the powers that be are pulling me off."

"What's happened?"

"Someone firebombed the house of the Chief of Police."

"Is he okay?"

"Yeah. The whole family got out, but they want all available detectives on duty."

"Especially their best one," I said.

"Flattery will get you everywhere. I'll be back at some point to sleep, but don't wait up. We'll still have a guy in a car out here."

"Tell him to come in for coffee and bathroom breaks."

"Will do. This might be the same group. Who knows?" He ran to his car.

I found myself hoping that the skinhead group was responsible. It would mean that every law enforcement official, prosecutor, judge, and probation officer would be on this until resolution. I shuddered at the thought of Chief Knight's house burning down. These idiots sure knew how to get the whole city up in arms.

As I wandered out to my shop to clean up after our project, I saw a squad pull into the driveway. It was a tan St. Louis County squad like the one Diane used, but she wasn't driving it. The male officer was tall and wiry with a pencil-thin moustache and aviator sunglasses.

He moved fast as he exited the squad. "Stay here."

It always pisses me off when cops treat me like a common citizen. I have nearly the same training they do, yet they always forget that. It was one thing to have Nate as a babysitter, but I didn't even know this control freak.

"What's happening?"

"The trip line went off. I'll check it out."

I was nervous about him going in alone, but I stayed put as he approached the woods. This wasn't at all how this operation was supposed to happen. With his gun out, he motioned with his hand for me to tuck further behind the house. I was clearly out of the line of sight from where I knew the tripod was set up, but I complied.

I waited for an eternity before he walked back out of the woods. "Nothing. Probably a deer."

"What took you so long?"

"I had to re-string the lines."

"Oh, that's good." I reminded myself to be grateful for the protection. "Need a coffee break?"

"Sure."

I left him on the porch while I brewed up a pot of French press. He took it to go and went back to his post. He wasn't a talkative fellow, and the silence between us was awkward. I didn't push him.

Returning to the shop, I let my mind process our situation while I worked. I had no idea why I would be the target of a killer. Maybe someone was trying to deliver a message to me to stay the hell away from the Jones family.

That made me think of Brian. He was locked up in detention again after the night of stealing bicycles. That wouldn't help his case at trial.

I realized that I would be forced to reassign him to another PO because of my involvement in his father's case as well as to mitigate the threat against me and Zoey. That saddened me. It seemed like a step toward leaving a job I loved, choosing safety over the good that I might be able to accomplish with someone like Brian.

I reflected that the kids were why I clung so fiercely to my job. I was in a position to pick and choose which kids to work with, and they usually ended up being the ones who got into my heart. I had begun not only to care about Brian but also to see how I could help him. While I was concerned about his father's influence, I thought that Brian harbored pro-social values that I could use as a starting point. He definitely exhibited common sense. Not all kids do. Not many adults do, for that matter.

Struggling with the decision about which probation officer would be best for Brian, my eyes surveyed the stains in my shop. I chose a honey oak tint for the Adirondack. Some people just let cedar gray naturally with age, but I prefer to preserve the wood's reddish hue. Sometimes I mix the stains to find just the right tone. I love working with wood, and I love building. I also love my work in probation.

What if I left my career and went into business with Kathy? If carpentry became my job rather than a hobby, would it stop being fun for me? What would I lose if I gave up working in probation? Would I be giving up too much of myself? Would Zoey really ask that of me? Kathy would in an instant, but would Zoey?

Then I realized that I had to own my decision. I didn't want to end up resenting Zoey for forcing my hand, and I couldn't make her wait too long while I tried to make up my mind. She was clearly hoping that we could have a different kind of life together.

I would have to be like the wood stain—preserving the best in my life and acting on my own highest values. It was up to me. My friends and Zoey wouldn't abandon me if I kept my job, but I would have to face the fallout if anyone got hurt. I had to make the right decision in light of what could happen to her or to me because of my work. I was driven to try to preserve the good in juveniles who veered off track and adults caught up in addiction, but I was also desperate to keep Zoey safe. I still didn't know what to do.

At least I could be decisive about one thing. I settled on Karen as the probation officer for Brian. I knew it was outside of the rules for me to choose who would get him. They were assigned on a rotation. But I couldn't help myself. Karen would be able to connect with him and build on his strengths. And I also knew she would keep me informed about his progress.

Chapter 16

ON THE TEN O'CLOCK NEWS, we learned that a judge's house had also been firebombed. The coverage showed firefighters losing ground on a house in the Hunter's Park area. The reporter didn't mention any casualties, but she also didn't mention that the occupants had gotten out safely. I assumed that meant someone was hurt or seriously injured, and they couldn't release details until the family was notified.

Nate came in around three in the morning and was up and out the door by eight on Tuesday. Grateful for breakfast, he had no progress to relate. I was starting to worry about him. He seemed to be sleeping even less than I was.

When I broached the subject of staying home another day, Zoey gave me a wounded look. *Her work shouldn't be overshadowed by the troubles in mine.* I got her message loud and clear. The thought that she might be safer at the university rather than in my vicinity helped convince me that we were doing the right thing. Zoey and I hardly spoke as we headed off to work in separate vehicles.

In the office, a sense of doom lingered in the air. What was happening to the pillars of our community? I longed to call Nate, but I knew he was up to his eyeballs trying to gain a foothold on the investigation. The pressure coming at him from this case must have been staggering.

I checked in with Karen about taking on Brian as a client, and she agreed. We discussed the importance of giving him space and building a good connection before pushing for results.

Luckily, Lou stopped in to give me an update.

"Can you believe it?" he inquired.

"Gutsy."

"Stupid, if you ask me. Could they think of a better way to bring every enforcement agency in the region down on them?"

"Stupid and bold. Any leads?" I pried.

"Not a one. They're still canvassing the neighborhood near the Chief's house, but it's a big piece of property, and the nearest neighbors are shielded by woods."

"You think this skinhead group did it?"

"I don't know. Could be. It took a group to hit both the Chief's house and the judge's. They were planning something big. We do know that."

"So how did they hurl the firebombs?"

"We aren't sure. Could have been thrown from a car, but no one saw or heard a car, so the perps might have been on foot. They used some kind of volatile cocktail in a glass container with a burning wick. They threw a couple to make sure one stayed lit."

"Pretty risky! Could one have exploded in their hands?"

"I don't really know. Probably. You know about as much about this stuff as I do, Jo."

"So, when are you done with the police consultation?" I couldn't see how his continued involvement would help, and I was worried about his safety.

"Today was my last day. Still have a job for me?"

"Always, Lou." As the leader of our intensive unit and a fantastic mentor to new staff, Lou's value to my department was without question. I finally convinced our chief that we should incorporate a training rate into his salary every time he trained in a new PO. He wasn't showing any signs of wanting to move out of the unit despite the night and weekend work, but I was doing everything in my power to offer incentives for senior staff to stay put. It made my job a lot easier.

When Zoey and I got home from work, we stayed in the house to be on the safe side. I was beginning to think that these precautions were pointless, now that the skinheads had moved on to higher targets.

Nate rolled in around eight o'clock looking haggard. He still didn't have any leads on the fire-starters. After asking us if we still needed him to keep staying overnight, he went right down to bed. While he might enjoy our company and Zoey's cooking, the extra drive was taking a toll on him. We assured him that we would be all right if the guard could stay on duty.

Chapter 17

ANOTHER DAY WENT BY with no further threats directed at me. After so many days of lying low, I was feeling antsy, and so were my dogs. I asked Zoey if she thought it would be okay for me to take the dogs out on the trail. She gave me her consent but insisted on going with us.

Before the walk, I forwarded the house phone to my cell. We were three quarters of the way along the trail when it rang. The caller I.D. read my home phone number, since the call was forwarded, so I couldn't tell who was calling.

After my initial greeting of "Hello," I received no response. I tried two more hellos before tuning in to listen. The sound of light breathing made my skin crawl; I listened even closer for background noise. When I heard nothing, I hung up. The light breathing made my mind flash to the sex offender shimmying down the neighboring brick building near work. He certainly would enjoy invading my privacy. Why hadn't I considered him as a possible voyeur before?

I asked Zoey to finish the walk without me and made my way as slowly and silently as I could to the tripod area. I got within fifty feet of it before sitting on a fallen log in an area of thick brush. I calmed my breathing and waited. I had a gut feeling that the stalker had called to determine if I was home before resuming his or her post behind my house. I knew my plan of approaching the area on my own was potentially dangerous, but I convinced myself that I would be stealthily quiet and just watch.

Once I squatted down, though, I realized that my plan had a flaw. If I didn't return in a timely manner, Zoey would worry. She would either call in the cavalry or come looking for me herself. I couldn't risk it.

As I made up my mind to go back home, I heard someone approaching from the southeast. The damp spring ground muffled the person's footfalls, but someone was definitely coming. So much for Nate's string warning system. It must have fallen to the ground.

I took out my cell and texted Zoey, "In the woods. Don't worry. Will send 10-min. updates." For me to use text messaging is rare, but it does have its place. I tried to remain totally quiet as the figure came into view. I could see a person dressed in camo. from head to toe and wearing a ski mask. The person was close to six feet tall, weighing 170 to 180 pounds. That's all I could tell. Ski mask pulled a portable chair and a camera out of a backpack. I was happy to see that it wasn't a video camera.

Opening my phone again, I texted Zoey, "I'm fine. He's here with a camera. Call 911. I'm not moving." I hoped Zoey had her phone on. I tried to stay still, focused on discovering anything that might be useful in identifying the person. At one point, his eyes turned in my direction, and I completely froze. I couldn't see a gun, but I would've bet that he had one. After a few seconds, he looked away. Eventually, I could hear a siren moving closer. The watcher got up, quickly stowed the chair, and ran southeast. I called Zoey and relayed the information.

"Don't chase him!" she yelled. "I'll get the guard to go after him."

I stayed where I was. The cop would use the tripod as a starting point for the chase. When the officer got to me, I simply pointed him in the direction the stalker had run.

Thinking about the person as a stalker gave me pause. *Could that have been Diane?* I searched my memory banks, now angry with myself for not thinking of her as a suspect. Perhaps I had clouded my perceptions by assuming that the person who was using the tripod was the same person who had chased me in the Camry. I'd also assumed that the stalker was a man. I couldn't remember a single distinguishing characteristic of the person in the ski mask that would indicate one gender over the other. Was he/she too slim to be the sex offender? Mack was pretty chunky. I was sure this person was taller and thinner.

When I made my way back to the house, Zoey was waiting for me.

"I was so stupid to let you do this," she said.

"Let me?"

"You know what I mean. At the very least, I should have been with you."

"I followed a hunch. I doubt either of us believed anyone would actually show up. It was a long shot. I'm going to check the caller I.D. in the house."

The call registered as an unknown caller. I told Zoey about my second hunch that the person might be Diane.

I didn't tell her about the sex offender. As much as I wanted to be completely honest with her, I worried that too much information about my unsavory work encounters with Mack would be too much for her, given the way our weekend had turned out.

"Could be her," Zoey agreed. "Either she's decompensating—you know, escalating in her focus on you—or she has talked herself into thinking she's looking out for you."

"With a camera?"

"Every job has to have one fringe benefit," she shrugged.

I felt glad she was able to joke about the Diane situation. We were way beyond any of our ex-girlfriends being a threat to our relationship. That made me smile.

"Seriously, though, I think you're right. She wasn't the person who followed us earlier, but the tripod set-up could be hers."

"I'm afraid to call Nate to update him. I don't want him to feel like he has to come back. Poor guy is worn thin."

"I'm sure he'll hear about it, and then he'll be pissed at you for not calling him." Zoey had a bad habit of usually being right.

"I'll call him later."

The responding cop knocked on the door. "No luck. Lost track of him." He was no more talkative than the first time we'd met.

I didn't tell him about my suspicion that it might be Diane, as he was a Deputy from the County—one of her peers.

I called Nate and gave him the update. He sounded distracted and down. He offered to come back out to stay with us, but I reassured him that the security system was working, and he sounded glad to be off the hook.

On Thursday, I checked in with Karen about Brian. She had seen him twice, once in detention and a second time in her office when he was released again. He was sullen and non-communicative. She planned to give him some space and to slowly try to connect with him.

That evening, I got home before Zoey, and as I walked into the house, I sensed that something was off. The hair stood up on the back of my neck. Stopping inside the door, I listened. No sounds whatsoever emerged above the ticking of the clock in the kitchen and the hum of the refrigerator. Sniffing the air, I detected a smell that I couldn't quite place. I stood still for another moment listening before calling out.

When nothing stirred, I ventured around the house, looking for a sign of intrusion. In our bedroom, the smell became stronger. I still couldn't place it. *Maybe some kind of perfume or lotion?* My top dresser drawer was open, and it looked as though someone had gone through it. The bedspread had a slight ripple on my side. I picked up my pillow. It emitted the same strange scent. I ripped the pillowcase off and hurled it across the room. *What the fuck?* A cold fury traveled up my spine.

I moved into the kitchen and reheated a cup of my morning pot of coffee before going out to the porch to wait for Zoey. I sat in the hanging swing chair, but I didn't feel like swinging. She looked concerned as she walked up.

"What's up, babe?" She came up to me and touched my knee, making small circles with her finger on the material of my pants.

"Someone's been in our house. In our bedroom."

Zoey blinked twice. "How could you tell?"

"Nothing's broken, but someone went into our bedroom, and I'm pretty sure the intruder went through my underwear drawer." I paused before saying, "Whoever it was touched my pillow." I waited for what I said to sink in.

"Did you call the police?"

"They're busy."

"Did the person break in?" She reached for my hand.

"Not that I could see, but I haven't checked all the doors and windows."

"Could we, please? I need to know."

"Sure, hon." She took my cup and helped me out of the chair. We moved from room to room. All of the doors were locked, and the security code hadn't been tripped. When we finished, I pulled out my phone and called Nate. He told me to change my security code in case the trespasser had somehow broken the code. While changing the password, I realized that using my dog's name was probably too obvious. After talking it over with Zoey, I set it to her childhood phone number's last four digits. Then I joined her in the living room, wishing we'd installed curtains to block the large windows.

I paced the floor, trying to contain my mounting rage. "I've had it with Diane."

"You think she was here?"

"Who else?" I looked at her for an answer.

"I don't know. What are we going to do?" Zoey placed her hands on her hips.

"We?"

"Yes, we." She looked me in the eyes.

"I'm going to confront her. Get this thing out in the open."

"Where are you thinking about doing this?"

"Haven't thought that far ahead yet."

"Promise you'll let me help."

I nodded. "I'm thinking I'll call her tomorrow and set up a meeting at a public coffee shop, presumably to talk to her about the Jones thing."

"She'll come for sure if she thinks you're asking her to help you."

"Then we have a plan."

"What about Nate?"

"He's still slammed by the arson cases."

"It's only fair to let him know what's going on."

"I'll send him an email."

Chapter 18

THE FOLLOWING DAY, I placed a call to Diane's cell phone. She readily agreed to meet me after work at Ground Under. I stayed busy throughout the day reviewing violation reports, signing warrants, and attending agency planning meetings, so I didn't think much about what I would say to Diane. When I did think about it, I remembered the smell on my pillowcase and got pissed off all over again.

I got to Ground Under early and secured a table in the back that afforded some privacy. Diane arrived early as well. I tried to make small talk until Zoey arrived. As soon as she saw Zoey, Diane stiffened and looked annoyed. Once we were all seated with our coffee, I said what I came to say.

"Diane, I want you to stop having anything to do with this Jones thing."

"Why?" she demanded.

"I think you're too invested."

"Invested is good."

"Not that invested. Did you enter my house yesterday?"

"Of course not." She answered too quickly.

"Well, I've changed the security code, and if I see you anywhere near my house, I'm going to get a protection order against you."

"I haven't done anything wrong. I've been protecting you, and this is the thanks I get?" She stood up to leave, waiting for me to apologize.

"Consider yourself warned. If you don't back off and you go near my house, it could cost you your job."

"I took a bullet for you," she said as she stormed out.

I looked at Zoey and was about to ask her thoughts on the interaction when Diane came back to the table. I stood up, ready for a physical fight, and so did Zoey.

"The person who's stalking you…is the same person who shot at me. Any rookie investigator would be able to make that connection. And it couldn't have been me. You think you know what this is about? When you get it through your thick head that I've been protecting you, give me a call. I have the information you need." She walked quickly out the door.

When she was gone, Zoey said, "While I think that needed to happen, what if it wasn't her?"

"It was her," I fumed.

"How do you know?"

"It was her smell."

Zoey shook her head. "Spooky. A stalker with police training and a license to carry a gun."

Once home, we walked the dogs. Then I made steaks on the grill, and over dinner we talked about the situation. *Was the Jones threat gone? Were the firebombs connected to the skinhead gang?*

I believed Diane's job meant enough to her that she would take my warning seriously, but Zoey thought Diane was in too deep to back off. I couldn't make heads or tails of what information she might be concealing to try to stay connected to the case and to me. Not for a millisecond was I considering calling her to find out.

I decided that I would set up a video camera that could record for up to ten hours, to capture any activity in our bedroom when we went to work each day. If someone was stalking me, I would fight back by using surveillance, too. The involvement of the sex offender was still a possibility, and I wanted proof that the person was indeed Diane.

Most of all, I wanted my life to go back to being predictable again.

Diane's final demand that I call her if I wanted to know the identity of the Camry driver was a compelling lure. I couldn't believe her, though. She had followed us to Ely, and she had been in our house. She could even have been photographing us from the tripod in the woods. I trusted that Zoey was right about Diane's obsession with me. I made a mental note to listen to Zoey in the future about all matters pertaining to whackos.

Chapter 19

"WHERE WERE YOU LAST NIGHT?"

The two detectives who showed up at my door the next morning were cold and distant. I invited them in and offered to brew up some coffee. They came in but declined my offer.

"What time?"

"Start from 3 p.m."

"I was at my desk until 4:30. Then I met Assistant Deputy Diane Anderson at Ground Under at around five. My partner, Zoey, was there, too." They looked at each other.

"Then we went home, had dinner, and stayed in all night."

"Was Zoey with you all night?"

"Yes. What's this about?"

"Diane is dead," said the taller one, glancing at his partner as if to signal that he would take the lead in this interview.

I sat there in shock for a second. "And you think I had something to do with this?"

"You are a person of interest."

"Where's Nate?"

"He's not in on this, and he can't help you here."

"But he knows what's going on. What happened to Diane?"

"Let's go down to the station and talk about it. Where can we find Zoey?"

"She went into work to catch up on her research."

"Where?"

"At Duluth University, Psychology Department." My interrogator looked at his partner again, but I couldn't fathom the mental signals he was sending this time. On the way to the station, he called another detective, giving Zoey's location.

When we got to the station, they sat me in an interrogation room and left me there for half an hour. I knew they were watching me from outside the one-way mirror.

Sending telepathic thoughts to Zoey to stay calm, I reassured myself that this would obviously work out. How could they seriously think that I had something to do with Diane's death?

Once they finally came into the room, one of the detectives offered me a cup of bad coffee, which I gladly accepted, and then they grilled me at length about my history with Diane. I filled them in up to the present time, including my suspicion that Diane had broken into my house.

When it became clear that they still thought I was involved, I invoked my Fifth Amendment rights and asked to speak to a lawyer. This cemented their stance about my guilt, and they left the room again.

A few minutes later, they offered me a phone call, which I promptly placed to my friend Linda at the County Attorney's office. I got her voice mail.

"Linda, it's me, Jo. I'm at the DPD being questioned in a murder investigation. I've requested an attorney. I know you can't represent me, but I need you to contact the best criminal lawyer you know and send him down here ASAP. I didn't do this, but they're intent on believing I did."

After an hour and another two cups of bad coffee, Rena Waters walked in. Shocked to see a public defender, I also knew that Linda wouldn't steer me wrong. If anyone would know the best criminal lawyer in Duluth, it would be the Chief Prosecutor.

She shook my hand, sat down, and asked me what I had told the police. I filled her in on everything that had happened, assured her of my innocence, and told her I was pretty sure they were questioning Zoey. Rena immediately got up to intervene. When she returned, she told me that Zoey had been cooperating. Rena had advised her to remain silent and told the police that if Zoey wasn't under arrest, she should be free to leave. When I heard that Zoey had been released, I breathed a relieved sigh and sat back in the chair.

"So, what's next?"

"We do the same for you."

"But why are they so focused on us?"

"You were the last people seen with her, and you had motive."

When I looked confused, she went on to explain.

"Maybe you killed her to stop the stalking. You threatened her."

"Threatened her how?"

"Witnesses at the coffee shop said you had a semi-heated exchange."

"I only told her that I would go after her job if she didn't back off."

"They have evidence that ties you to the crime."

"What evidence?"

"It's a stretch for sure. They found motorcycle tracks to and from her house and a compromising picture of you and Diane on the ground near the body."

"That can't be. I haven't been involved with her for ten years. Where was the body?"

"I'm not going to give you any more facts. They might assume you have intimate details because you were there."

"Right." I scratched my head. "Well, let them take tire impressions and match them to my bike. They'll see that the treads aren't a match. End of their theory. Then they can go out and find out who did this."

"Do you have any ideas?"

"I really didn't know her that well, but there's a chance this could be tied to a juvenile I was working with. His father is part of a white supremacy ring in Duluth, and the members have been following and threatening me. Diane got a hero complex going and tried to step in to protect me. Those guys are not to be messed with. Nate, err… Jerome Nathan, will probably have a theory on that." I nodded for emphasis. "He's looking into the firebombings. I wouldn't be surprised if this wasn't the work of the same group."

"I'll have my investigator look into it."

"So, you have a private practice in addition to being a public defender?"

"Absolutely. Don't worry. We'll get to the bottom of this."

"Am I in custody?"

"No. Let's get out of here."

As we were about to leave, the deputies came back in with their handcuffs out, read me my Miranda rights, and took me into custody on the charge of murder in the first degree. Rena stopped everything and demanded an explanation.

"We just came from your house, Supervisor Spence. We found the saw."

"What saw?" I couldn't follow what they were talking about.

"The one you used to cut off her hand."

I sat down hard. My head spun. I couldn't catch my breath. "What are you saying?"

"We found her hand buried in your yard."

Rena stepped up into the detective's face. "This is a clear frame-up. Any idiot could see that. Do your job, or I'll have it. You think my client threatened Diane in public, left a picture of herself with the deceased at the scene as well as motorcycle tracks, then hid evidence in clear sight of her home? You're either stupid or desperate."

"It wasn't in clear sight."

"But easy to find." He grimaced a bit.

"Put Nate on this. He'll get to the bottom of it," I blurted.

"Nate is your friend. He's off the case."

"But he knows about the Jones connection. Talk to him about it. Diane knew who was following me. Maybe the stalker killed her to silence her."

They looked at me like my statement was a convenient fabrication and escorted me out of the interrogation room and into a squad. I was booked into the jail, strip searched, and placed in a private cell. During the booking process, it wasn't lost on me that Diane was employed by the Sheriff's Department. *One of their own.*

Chapter 20

ALSO APPARENT WAS THAT my previous trips to the jail throughout my career meant nothing. I was just another criminal now. When I caught sight of Gerri, someone I had known for quite awhile, she looked surprised but didn't offer any words of support.

At least I had my own cell. PO's don't always fare so well in jail. They're viewed by the other prisoners as part of the system that caused their incarceration. The pigs and the system were responsible for their imprisonment rather than anything they did themselves.

I alternated between pacing my cell and lying on my cot thinking about what I could do to clear myself. I knew I'd be arraigned within seventy-two hours. The police would need seventy of those hours to pull charges together in a case of this magnitude.

When my lunch arrived, I looked at it skeptically. In the jail, clients cooked the meals under the supervision of kitchen staff. They didn't know who would be getting which plate, so there was little chance anyone had spit in it or worse. I couldn't go without eating for long, so I ate what I could of the bland mac & cheese, a slice of Wonder bread, and a glob of canned fruit. The fare reminded me of school lunch.

I sent some mental thoughts Zoey's way to let her know I was okay. She had obviously told the truth—that we had spent the entire night together. Did they suspect her of being my accomplice? I hoped they would take tire impressions of my motorcycle, thereby eliminating my bike. Whoever set me up couldn't fake that. Maybe there were fingerprints on the saw. *A saw. Diane's hand had been cut off.* I felt bad for her. As angry as I had been about her invading my home, I didn't wish her dead. *They can't possibly believe me capable of*

103

that. But they did. Even with a terribly obvious frame-up. My mind wouldn't stop. It was like one song playing over and over again on a record.

I paced. Finally, when I couldn't stand my own thoughts anymore, I forced myself to meditate. I lay down on the bunk, closed my eyes, and envisioned sitting on the floor with Zoey in front of the fireplace. She looked into my eyes, and I could feel how much she loved me. I imagined her reaching for my hand and entwining her fingers into mine, her eyes steady and strong, never losing faith in me. "I love you, Jo. And we're in this together."

I kept my mind there for as long as I could before coming back to the cold reality of my cell. I never liked the smell of jails, a rank combination of male sweat, Lysol, and human desperation, and now it would be forever seared into my brain.

I made up my mind that thinking obsessively about my plight was getting me nowhere. I devised a plan. Each time I started to think obsessively, I would do ten pushups, then meditate and focus on something nurturing. I was in a hot tub with Zoey, riding on my motorcycle, walking in the woods with my dogs.

My arms were starting to tire, and I still couldn't clear my mind. I conjured up Kathy and Donna, my best friends in the Valley, as well as Sandy and Ree from Big Noise, all of us together playing cards and drinking coffee. Suddenly I was jerked from my meditation by the voice of a guard.

"Visitor."

I jumped up, thankful for the interruption in my mental gymnastics. I was escorted out to the booking area where professional visits occurred. All visits were recorded unless they were between a lawyer and his or her client. As I walked in, I saw Nate. My heart leapt, and I resisted the urge to hug him.

"Hey, buddy," he said.

I nodded and smiled. "I'm so glad you see it that way. I thought you were banned from my presence."

"I'm not working on your case. I'm here on the Jones matter. We're making some progress on tying his group to the arson cases. These guys aren't that sophisticated."

"What do you have?"

"They used a rudimentary incendiary device. We're getting warrants to search for the materials. We also have a security camera from the judge's house and a rough I.D. on the perps. They were definitely skinheads. They wore masks, but we could see some of their tattoos. It's only a matter of time until we catch one of them. This is potentially a federal offense, so we have leverage to turn them against their brothers."

"As in Jones?" I wondered about the influence these creeps had had on Brian. All of the kids we deal with are important, but this kid had gotten under my skin. I knew instinctively that he wasn't too far gone.

"Maybe, or brother gangsters."

"How can I help?"

"Did Diane do anything to piss them off?"

"I don't know, but I wouldn't doubt it. She probably thought that if she was the hero in getting them arrested, I'd be forever grateful. Who knows what she was capable of or even into for that matter. You know what I know. You should ask Zoey. She might be able to profile it for you."

"We have a profiler working on it, but bringing Zoey in wouldn't hurt. Maybe I'll have them talk to each other."

"Where is Zoey? Is she okay?" I leaned in, wanting to know this more than anything we'd talked about. A part of me was off balance, being so effectively removed from her.

"She's at Kathy and Donna's. She's freaked out but okay. She's smart enough to know that we'll figure this out."

"Are they making any progress?"

"I can't talk about that."

"Where did they find the aaah…?"

"The hand?"

"Yes."

"Can't say that, either. They might make the assumption that you knew the answer because you put it there. The less you know the better."

"But how can I help myself if I don't know how to unravel this thing?"

"You need to trust that we'll get to the bottom of it."

"They have their minds made up. They have me. They aren't looking for the killer. They won't even let you help." My voice rose. A guard peered into the visiting room. Nate placed a hand on my shoulder.

"I can't imagine what you must be going through, Jo, but hang on. You can't do anything from in here."

"I can't work on it. You can't work on it. How the hell are we going to straighten this out?"

"Jo, they're bringing in the FBI and the BCA because of our conflict of interest. We hate when they come into our jurisdiction, but at the same time, they know what they're doing. They've brought in a prosecutor from a neighboring county, too. You're too well known around here. Everyone's watching this."

"Has anyone told you that Diane said she knew who was following me?"

"They wrote that off to you deflecting blame."

"What if it's true?"

"Trust that they will track down every lead."

"You believe I didn't make it up?" I had to hear him say it.

"Don't even question that, Jo."

"That's what I love about you, Nate."

"That's why I'm off the investigation."

I told Nate about my method for survival involving the pushups and meditations. He laughed and said he'd have a talk with the jailers to see if they couldn't keep me in coffee. He knew that if I didn't have at least four cups a day, I'd go through serious withdrawal. I did have a headache but hadn't made the connection.

Chapter 21

Somehow, I got through my seventy-two-hour hold without going insane. At the arraignment hearing, they didn't parade me in with the other prisoners, but waited until all of the other hearings concluded.

When I was finally led into the courtroom in my orange jumpsuit, handcuffs, and shackles, I caught sight of Zoey's shocked reaction to my appearance. I knew I looked terrible. All of my friends were there, and my dad and step-mom had flown in from Florida. They all put on brave faces and smiled at me as I entered.

Rena met me on the left side of the courtroom. Of all my many court appearances, that was a spot I had never occupied. A County Attorney whom I had never met stood on the right. A judge that I didn't recognize sat atop the bench.

The judge cleared his throat. "We'll go on the record in the matter of Jo Spence. Murder in the First Degree. Ms. Spence, how do you plead?"

Rena spoke on my behalf. "Not guilty, your honor."

The judge didn't even look at me. "The matter will be set for an omnibus hearing. It has to go in front of me." He looked at the clerk.

"June 15, 2 p.m."

"We request R.O.R., your honor." Rena jumped in without prompting.

"I'm getting to that." The judge intoned. He looked at the prosecutor.

"This is murder one, your honor. We request that she be held without bail."

The judge allowed the defense to argue. "My client is a respected Probation Supervisor, your honor, with an impeccable employment history, and she's an upstanding citizen. The case has holes in it big enough to drive a truck through. We request that she be released on her own recognizance, or at a minimum, allowed bail or supervised release."

"Your honor, she can't be released to staff she has managed," the prosecutor argued.

"That's discriminatory. She's entitled to all the legal benefits available to any other citizen. I've read through the complaint. The evidence is overwhelming, albeit perhaps too much so. I'm setting bail at three hundred thousand. If Ms. Spence makes bail, I'm adding a condition that she report to a federal probation officer under pre-trial release. She most certainly does not oversee them, and they are right across the street."

The crowd burst into a loud murmur. The judge simply walked out. Rena leaned into me. "Can you make bail?"

"Is ten percent cash bond an option?"

"No."

"Wow, that's a lot to come up with, but I'm sure my friends and family will help."

"Okay, then. Call me when you're out."

I turned to look at Zoey. She mouthed, "We've got this." And I was led away.

I sat in holding with three other females while waiting to be transported back up to the jail. I was numb and in shock. I guess I had assumed that the charges would be cleared by the time of my arraignment hearing. The holding cell had vulgarities and angry anti-system phrases etched into the walls and benches. I made a mental note to have the work crew paint the cells once I got out.

One woman in holding had me on edge. Large and rough looking, she was peering at me like I was a candy bar for quick consumption. When I asked her what she was in for, she responded, "Unpaid traffic tickets. A lot of them. What about you?"

We were both shocked when I responded that I was in for murder.

When I got back up to the jail, I was housed with the general population. Apparently, word had gotten out about what I was in for, and the other inmates gave me a wide berth. My head still pounded, but I thought the caffeine withdrawal was easing up a bit. I sat alone in my cell, which bordered the common area in the Delta pod, and looked out the window. I could see deer grazing at the edge of the clearing on the north side of the building. It made me think of home. In that moment, I fully understood what the term heartache meant. Dinnertime came, without a word from anyone.

I finally walked out into the common area and began a game of solitaire in front of the TV. The news came on, and everyone in the room stopped what they were doing and looked at me. The evening news covered the story about me being held in connection to the brutal murder and dismemberment of Assistant Deputy Diane Anderson. The report also mentioned that I was a probation officer. After they flashed a picture of me, I looked around the room and felt hostility coming from everyone, including the guards. I quietly got back up and went back to my cell. So far, I did not have a cellmate.

I found a book to read but couldn't concentrate. While I knew Zoey was furiously working to get the bail together, I couldn't imagine what the barriers were. At around eight in the evening, the guard told me I had a visitor. I was led into a no-contact visiting area where Plexiglas separated inmates from outsiders. Zoey had finally come. To see me walk into that tiny room in my orange prisoner scrubs must have been really difficult for her. I plastered a smile on my face to lighten the mood. We both picked up our phone handsets and sat down facing each other.

"Hi, hon."

She smiled at me. "Be strong, babe."

"Have to," I said.

"We're working on your bail."

"I had no doubt. What's the prognosis?"

"We're close to having the full amount in cash. It was quicker than putting up K & D's house as collateral." When she saw my eyebrows knit together, she went on to explain, "Your house is in your name, and using that would take time. Your parents don't really have a big house anymore, but between all of us, we have close to the amount we need in cash. It's just a matter of getting the banks to part with it. Everything is coming together, but it's taking more time than I imagined. Maybe it might have been faster to put up the house."

"How much are you short?"

"Twenty-five thousand."

"I have about twelve in my savings. If you bring me a check, I'll write it.

I'm pretty sure I can get the money moved between accounts from here."

"Great! That leaves thirteen thousand."

"Have you talked to Nate?"

"He chipped in seven thousand already. We're having a fundraiser tomorrow with some local singers. You know, The Three Altos? They're doing a benefit concert for you at Leif Ericson Park. I'm sure the whole lesbian community of Duluth will show up."

"The ones who think I'm innocent, anyway."

She smiled at me through the glass, putting her hand up to it. I reached up and placed my palm on the glass across from hers.

"God, I miss touching you," I said.

"You'll be out soon, hon."

"Sell my Range Rover at the fundraiser if you want. Put it up for auction. That should pull in a few thousand. Remember, it has a rebuilt motor. I need to get something with better MPG, anyway."

"The pups miss you," she said into the phone. "Cocoa has been climbing right up into my lap. She's a big dog for that."

"I miss you all so bad."

"Have you heard anything new on the case?" She still had her hand aligned with mine on the Plexiglas.

"No. Nate can't work on it. I can't work on it. They're bringing in the FBI. That could be good, I guess. I have to believe that they'll find out who did this. I mean, I'd go crazy if I thought people could be so easily convinced that I'm a killer. My name has been plastered all over the news."

"Hon, people who know you, we know the truth."

"My reputation has been shot all to hell."

"We'll figure this out."

We talked for an hour about what it was like in jail and about what everyone else had been up to. She said my parents were livid that anyone could even think I had anything to do with this. They had tried to go on TV to defend me. Long and short of it was—she thought I'd be out by Thursday morning, as soon as the fundraiser was over and the bail bondsperson could meet her at the jail.

I slowly made my way into the jail population over the next day. I went out for recreation in the gym with the other women. One of them came up to me and gave me a shoulder bump while we walked the perimeter of the gym, saying "Dyke PO bitch" under her breath.

"Correct on all counts," I said in reply. "One who is not to be fucked with." I moved in front of her and stood my ground. Fortunately, I was a couple of inches taller than she was. I knew I had to stand up, or I'd be a target for more than one of them. Everyone in the gym watched the interaction. I had assumed a karate stance. I could only execute a few kicks, but she didn't know that. The guard jumped up and radioed in a code. The woman backed down and walked the other way. I ambled over to an exercise bike and hopped on. The guard cancelled the code.

After that, all I wanted to do was sleep. I couldn't stay awake at all. I slept through the afternoon and night. Morning eventually came, and I was told to prepare for court.

I showered, ate, and was driven in the van with the same woman who'd threatened me. I gave her my best *don't-fuck-with-me* stare, and she backed down again. I sat in holding until roughly 11 a.m. I was the last in-custody hearing of the morning.

My friends, family, and a lot of my staff sat in the spectator seats as I was brought in, shackled and cuffed. As my eyes scanned the courtroom, I caught sight of Mack near the back. He had on his favorite trenchcoat, with no shirt collar visible at his neckline. *What was he doing here?*

I stood by Rena.

"What's this about?" I whispered.

"I'm pretty sure they're dropping the charges."

"Go ahead, Mr. Donner." The judge nodded at the prosecutor.

"It's my understanding that new evidence may impact the charging of this case. We request a dismissal on all counts without prejudice at this time, your honor." Everyone in the courtroom burst into applause.

"Order. Order in the courtroom." Once things settled down, the judge continued. "I trust the defense has no objection?"

Rena turned to me with a smile. "No objection, your honor."

I turned to look at Zoey, and she mouthed. "I'll pick you up at the jail."

It took forever to process out. Zoey was waiting for me when I was released. I ran to her and pulled her into a huge hug. With my cheek resting against her shoulder and my face pressed into her neck, I breathed in and tried to absorb the pure joy of being close to her and feeling her skin against mine. I caught a whiff of the body wash she favored—Rain Bath by Neutrogena—a fragrance I loved so much that I had started to use it myself just to catch a hint of her at random moments throughout my day. The jail's Ivory soap had offered no such pleasant associations.

I didn't want to let go, but we eventually made it to the car and then home.

All of my friends were there as well as my dad and step-mom. They had questions, but I didn't have answers. We all drank coffee, ate cookies, and basked in the comfort of my freedom and our bond.

When everyone left, Zoey and I processed what had transpired in the preceding days. The detectives had questioned her a number of times. With another lawyer from Rena's private practice with her at all times, Zoey had patiently repeated her version of events, beginning with the Jones harassment all the way through learning that Diane had been stalking me, ending with the meeting at Ground Under.

I called Nate and invited him to come out to the house for dinner. Once we sat down to eat, he informed me that I wasn't out of the woods yet. Some of the detectives weren't convinced of my innocence. Their investigation was ongoing, but the evidence in my favor was piling up. They had compared the tire tracks at the scene to my cycle—not a match. The saw had a second blood type on it—a type that didn't match mine. The picture of Diane and me had Diane's fingerprints on it, but mine were not found. Also, the same two blood types were detected in minute blood spatter on the face of the photo. Nate said that the picture may not have been left intentionally. It had been found on the ground under Diane's body.

When Nate left, I called my boss at home to check on the status of my employment. He informed me that he had no doubts about my innocence but said that I was on paid administrative leave until the ethics committee could review the situation. It was standard for them to wait and see how an allegation panned out before publicly backing an accused employee. Lou called me around nine and told me that he was holding down the fort.

At the end of the night, I reveled in the comfort of my own bed with Zoey beside me. Cocoa and Java were Velcro, and I let them pile on top of us.

Chapter 22

ZOEY TRUDGED OUT TO HER CAR the next morning with a heavy heart, not wanting to leave me. She promised to call during her breaks before finally tearing herself away and heading to work. I walked the dogs on the trail. Then I let myself look around to see if I could determine where the police had found Diane's buried hand and the saw.

Perhaps just the idea of a dismembered body part on my land put me on edge. At any rate, I felt spooked. I shook off my jitters and headed out behind the house to the area where Diane had set up her surveillance spot. I thought I heard movement in the woods, but I didn't see anyone. When I touched the ground near the tripod, it felt warm to me. The smell of Diane lingered in the air.

I pulled out my cell and informed Nate. He called the FBI agent assigned to investigate the murder, and three agents showed up forty-five minutes later. The profiler remained at the house with me as the other two agents processed the scene. They were intrigued by the new development, and once they were all assembled at the house, the profiler began to question me.

"Ms. Spence, thank you for agreeing to speak with us." The situation reminded me of my interrogation before being booked for murder, but I tried to remain cooperative. I only wished that Zoey could have been there with me. If these officers could help solve the murder, it was worth talking with them.

"Thanks for coming out."

"I'm Vincent, and these two are Henry and Lisa."

Vincent was nondescript. He was medium everything. His one distinguishing feature was steely blue eyes that seemed to take in everything around him. Henry was tall and strong with wire-rimmed glasses more suited to a professor. Lisa, thin and brunette, moved like a gymnast, or a cat.

"Do you have any idea who would have been watching you?"

"No, I assumed earlier that it was Diane. Now this." I shrugged. "I suppose it could have something to do with the Jones thing. Do you think I'm in danger?"

"Could be," was all he said.

"You don't know?"

He nodded no. "Did Diane have a partner?"

"Do you mean life partner, or work partner?"

"Let's start with life partner."

"It never occurred to me. Maybe?" I searched my memory for any shred of evidence about a partner. "I didn't think so, but I made an assumption."

"Based on what?"

"All the time she put into trying to 'protect me,'" I said with some anger.

"I understand you believe she broke into your house."

"She did."

"How are you so sure of that?"

I told him about how the intruder left her cologne smell on my pillow. And then when I confronted Diane, I recognized it.

"Did she use that cologne when you dated her?"

"I can't remember. That was a long time ago." I hadn't recognized the scent in the house, but Diane had the same fragrance on when I met with her at Ground Under.

"How long?"

"Over ten years."

"And you haven't heard from her since?"

"Actually, I would from time to time. She always wanted to hook up. I wanted nothing to do with her. She kind of creeped me out. I didn't even know she still lived in town. Do you know exactly when she started working for the Sheriff's Department?" I looked at each of them.

"Roughly six months ago. She finished her training and was out on her own right before she met up with you."

"You must have been to her apartment. Was there any sign of a girlfriend?"

The officers all shifted and looked down at the ground, except the profiler, who watched me intently.

"What? What did you find?" It had to be significant.

"A shrine to you," he said, watching me closely.

I felt shocked. "A what?" I had heard him, but I needed time to digest what it meant.

"Pictures, news clippings; her computer was loaded with searches about you dating back to when you stopped seeing her."

"She fixated on me for ten years?" *Zoey was right.*

"It looks like it. Tell me what happened during the course of your dating."

"We dated for only a couple of months. It started out normally. You know, two people getting to know one another. Eventually, she kind of freaked me out. Got too intense. Clingy. It felt weird."

"How'd you end it?"

"I told her it wasn't working out. I didn't want to see her anymore."

"How'd she take it?"

"Not well. I couldn't shake her. I had to really set a limit."

"Then she left you alone?"

"No, I had to tell her a couple of times. She'd show up at social functions. Pretend like it was an accident. Then she'd act all weird. I told her to leave me alone, it's over."

"Did you ever sleep with her?"

"No, but I'm not answering any more of your questions if you're only interested in exploring my motives. I didn't kill her. The person who did might have been out in my woods just a little while ago. A murderer is still out there."

They remained unperturbed by this, but did offer to go out into the woods again to go over what had convinced me that my stalker was back. I gladly accepted. I knew they were seeing this as an opportunity to search without a warrant, but I didn't care. I needed to know what was happening on my property. I thought briefly about calling Rena, but then I shook off the idea.

They showed me where the hand had been buried and then revealed that the saw had been found in the garbage bin. We didn't find anything else disturbed, except that my motorcycle was missing. They informed me that it had been impounded for evidence. That broke my heart.

Chapter 23

MY MOTORCYCLE WAS IMPOUNDED, and Zoey had sold my Range Rover at auction. She said that an oddly cheerful, plump man named Mack had paid a generous amount for it. I stifled a groan and lied, "Ahh, that's great." I would have to call my boss and explain the conflict of interest—one that I didn't care to deal with right now. Best not to think about it too much.

My immediate problem was a need for wheels. I searched CraigsList for a Honda Silverwing GL 500 or 600 Interstate. There were two in the Twin Cities area, one in close-to-mint condition with only seven thousand miles on it. It had hard bags and a driver's backrest. I made a call and found that it was still available. The owner said that he'd bought it for his wife, but she never took to riding. He'd cleaned the carburetors, put new tires on it, and reupholstered the seat. It was driver ready, and for $2500 cash, he would meet me in Hinkley, and I could drive it home.

I called the lead FBI agent Vincent to tell him about my plans, and Kathy and I headed to my bank to get the cash. She gave me a lift to meet the seller, and I took the bike for a test drive. By the time Zoey got home, I was out front with my new ride, polishing it up and checking the fluids. I liked it even more than my original bike. This one was red and looked nearly flawless. The trunk lock worked, as did both of the hard saddlebags. They appeared to be original. It had cruise, and good tires.

Zoey took one look at it, shook her head, and wordlessly stroked the bags as she walked past and went into the house. I laughed and joined her. She knew me so well it was uncanny. What surprised me was that she said she wanted my old bike when we got it back.

I filled her in on the rest of the day's events, and although she didn't say it, I could tell that she felt disappointed to have missed out on seeing the profiler at work. I also told her about Diane's shrine. She didn't say "I told you so," but in fact, she had warned me. I wondered if somehow I could have prevented Diane's death if I had only listened to Zoey and taken action to address Diane's obsession earlier.

When I told Zoey about the return of the observer in the woods, she insisted that we call Nate.

"Hey, Jo, I'm almost there."

"I'll put on the coffee. Isn't this supposed to be your day off?"

"No such thing, I'm afraid."

We sat on the porch listening to the sounds of the birds making their new nests. The night was warm for spring. Zoey brought out a serving tray with coffee, cream, sugar, and some cookies. Rain clouds were moving in, and the air had the smell of lightning. The sky was darker than it should have been, and a slight purple cradled the gathering thunderclouds.

I was happy to be home, but somehow I felt numb. My numbness was probably protecting me to some degree from everything I had been through lately. Even my anger at how vulnerable I was to the unknown watcher felt muted.

Zoey spoke up. "Nate, are we in danger here?"

"Well, the offer for you both to come to my house still stands."

"What about work?" Zoey asked.

I instinctively moved to Zoey and put my arm around her.

She put her head on my shoulder. "I have to teach."

"Can you do most of it away from the U?"

"Most of it, but I have to make class and put in a respectable amount of office hours."

Nate said, "I'll check with my chief about assigning someone to shadow you at work."

"As in a guard?"

"As in a guard posing as a TA." Nate grinned, trying to reassure us. "And I'm moving back in."

Nate couldn't quite pull it off. He was up to his eyeballs in the other investigation, and bone tired, but he was digging down deep to try to look eager. He smiled and shrugged his massive shoulders.

We spent a quiet weekend together, although Nate spent much of it working in town. On Monday morning, Zoey got up early and made eggs, pancakes, and bacon for breakfast.

Nate wolfed down an impressive serving. "Now, this is what I call hazard pay."

We cleaned up the dishes while Zoey showered and dressed for work. Once they were all ready to go, they piled into Nate's butt-ugly Crown Victoria. I remained at home, still on leave and under suspicion, numbly waiting for Diane's killer to surface again.

Chapter 24

MY DAY SLIPPED AWAY. With so much guilt and anxiety weighing me down, I wasn't able to do anything productive. When the time for Zoey and Nate to come home neared, I managed to pull steaks out of a marinade of red wine vinegar, garlic, and olive oil. While the steaks were grilling, I sautéd a mushroom and onion sauce on the stove, and finished twice-baked potatoes. Then I cut veggies for a salad. That was all I could accomplish.

In contrast, Zoey arrived home like a woman on a mission. Once we slowed our eating enough to speak, she asked Nate if he wouldn't mind passing the evening by practicing defensive tactics with us. He eyed her suspiciously.

"I hope that means my nose and family jewels are off limits."

"Wouldn't touch them," Zoey smirked.

I had received a ton of training as a probation officer, but I thought doing the exercises would be a good way to feel like we were doing something proactive to protect ourselves. Nate and I planned what we would cover as we cleaned up the evening dishes.

First, Nate unloaded his gun and walked up to me with it pointed at my head. I practiced the evasion maneuver and twisted it out of his hand. Zoey took a little while to get the hang of it, but she repeated the skill until she could do it correctly three times in a row. Then he put each of us in a chokehold, and we did a shoulder shrug and slammed our arms down while twisting to break the hold.

In the classes I take that are designed for PO's, the trainers are usually quite gentle to avoid liability. It was helpful to practice on an oversized man like Nate who wouldn't be so gentle. I needed to know that these maneuvers would work in real-life situations. Even though I am five feet ten inches tall and in good physical health, most men of equal size are stronger, younger, faster, and sometimes on drugs, which inhibits their ability to sense pain, so I felt compelled to stay on top of my game. The current threats to Zoey and me added additional fuel to my efforts. In the final maneuver we practiced, Nate started out on top of me, pinning me to the ground. I couldn't escape his weight and strength and knew that I had to avoid being pinned at any cost. Zoey couldn't break the hold, either. Once we were done, Nate reminded us that knees, genitals, and eyes were the best targets.

"You have to inflict real pain to escape an attacker," he said. He reviewed several pressure points and strong-arm holds designed to take a perpetrator down to the ground for handcuffing.

The exercises had released some of our tension, and we felt more like ourselves again. We claimed our favorite spots in the living room until bedtime, watching mindless crime TV. Cocoa took a liking to Nate and snuggled against him on the couch with her head in his lap. Watching him contentedly petting her, I wondered if a permanent relationship wasn't too far off for Nate. I suspected his bachelor lifestyle would be lonely after his time guarding us. He caught me looking at him, smiled, and relaxed a little more into the couch.

During commercials, he updated me on the arson cases. He now referred to them as the Jones arson cases. The police had executed a search warrant at the Jones property. Ingredients for the incendiary devices were found in the garage and basement of the home. Technicians were analyzing all of it at the lab. Once the results were conclusive, Mr. Jones and the older boys would be arrested. Then the police would go to work trying to turn them on each other.

"What about Brian?" I asked. I knew that he had been released again and was living in the worst possible environment.

"So far, we have nothing that ties him to this."

I didn't particularly feel reassured. Even if the police didn't tie him to the arsons, I pondered what effect being a witness to these crimes was having on Brian. I was sure he knew about them. Hopefully, a part of him understood what harm was being done to real human beings. I wished I could be there for him, to remind him of a different future he could have.

Chapter 25

THE NEXT MORNING AT BREAKFAST, Zoey asked Nate if he would have time after work to teach her how to shoot. I jolted wide awake.

"What?"

"I want to learn how to shoot."

"Why?"

"Isn't that obvious?"

"You think that will help?"

"I can't sit around waiting for something to happen. I need to prepare. I mean, if this is what our lives are going to be like, I better adjust."

"A gun in the hands of an inexperienced shooter is more likely to be used against her." I knew I was quoting sterile and impersonal statistics, but I couldn't figure out what else to say.

"I don't plan to be inexperienced."

"Can we at least talk about this more?"

"We can talk all you want, but I'm learning to shoot. I may even buy a gun." With that, she was up and out the door, waiting at the car while I talked to Nate. He said we could all practice shooting after work, but he was staying out of the middle.

I spent a good part of the morning walking the dogs and readying my bike for a ride. It had rained a little the night before, but the clouds were clearing up. I changed the oil and cleaned the spark plugs. The bike really looked to be in top condition, so after lunch I took a drive along the north shore of Lake Superior. I had always planned to take a riding trip around it, and now that Zoey had expressed some interest in riding herself, I pictured us making the trip together, staying at campsites and hotels along the way.

My new bike rode perfectly. The backrest was definitely a plus I had never considered before. When I got home, I looked up several blogs about the Lake Superior circle tour online and printed out a potential itinerary to go over with Zoey. I needed to focus on a future that wasn't so out of control. Clearly, if something didn't change, Zoey would take charge of her own security.

I walked over to K&D's house along the river trail with my dogs. It took us a good hour. Kathy was happy to take a break, and we caught up on her designing/architecture projects and the status of my personal terror drama. She was still intent on convincing me to begin building green kitchens and bathroom projects for the houses she designed. When she wouldn't let up, I told her I'd help her out with one project while on leave if it worked out time wise. She said she'd see if she could set something up.

Zoey and Nate didn't arrive home until after seven. They walked in with take-out, and we ate out on the screen porch. Zoey ate quickly, informing me that she needed to change into suitable shooting clothes, and went into the house. Nate gave me a helpless shrug.

"She's definitely her own person," I said.

He agreed. "Coming with us?"

I nodded and found ear protection for everyone. Nate pulled paper targets from his trunk. We attached them to some logs, moved up to the deck, and started shooting. Zoey learned quickly how to sight and steady the semi-automatic pistol, which Nate had provided. By the end of the night, her bullet groupings were tight even when fired in succession. I had been through shooting 101, but rarely had time to practice, so I fired off a dozen or so rounds. Nate then instructed us on how to unholster the pistol, draw quickly, and fire.

While practicing, Zoey didn't smile and was focused like I'd never seen her before. Her intensity scared me a bit.

The silence between us was deafening, especially after the explosive sounds of guns going off. She was wound tight, and I didn't know how to change that. She retired to the bedroom with a book.

I dished up some ice cream and went out to the screen porch to think. The night was cool, and I could see stars. I breathed in fresh air and set the bowl down to let the ice cream soften as I pondered things. My relationship with Zoey was strained. My relationship with my friends was strained as well. An unknown person was stalking us. The stalking may or may not have been related to the arsons happening around town, which were evidently tied to the Jones skinhead group.

It pissed me off that Zoey, Kathy, and Donna blamed me for all of it. Like I somehow manufactured everything. I ate my ice cream by moonlight and finally went to bed at around 3 a.m.

The next day, Zoey was pleasant, but I knew our issues weren't resolved. After she left for work, I walked the dogs over to Kathy's house again. She had worked up a list of green building materials, suppliers, and rough pricing that we could use in our new endeavor. She showed them to me before placing a call to a contractor she knew who was working on one of her house designs. The crew hadn't begun on the kitchen yet, and she set up an appointment for the two of us to meet with the homeowner, who was totally fired up about the green kitchen idea.

She suggested that I could easily make Adirondack rockers out of a recycled plastic product that would go over big with the demographic she designed houses for. That little side business could fill in any gaps I might face in the "new enterprise" she planned for us. I got so caught up in her energy and enthusiasm, I nearly forgot that I already had a job and had only agreed to help her on one project.

Chapter 26

I WENT HOME, CLEANED the house with determination, left a note for Zoey, and then met Kathy at the Town Hall so we could ride to the client's building site together. The homeowner was eager to see the green ideas she had for his kitchen, and Kathy showed him three samples of countertops that were an amalgam of recycled products resembling granite. She then showed him energy-efficient lighting fixtures, cabinet products made from bamboo, and flooring samples from renewable woods and conglomerate tiles. The final cost was a couple thousand higher than his original design, but he jumped at it. He even ordered two of my rockers. I felt a little dizzy. This had all happened quickly, and I didn't even know how long my administrative leave would last.

When I got home, I updated Zoey on the project. Nate had dropped her off, eaten a baked cheese soufflé, and gone back into work. Zoey was thrilled with my plans. I could tell she had her hopes up about me quitting my job, and I didn't have the heart to bring her down. She really needed to have some light in her life after all I had put her through.

Evidence of her stress manifested in the pistol she had purchased, which was on the kitchen island in plain sight. It lay there between us screaming for attention, but I refused to acknowledge it. We did the dishes in silence and lounged in the living room with our books.

After about an hour of reading, I got up to use the bathroom. As I passed in front of a window overlooking the backyard, glass exploded in front of me. I felt something hot hit my face, and Zoey dove with me to the ground. The next thing I knew, she ran into the kitchen, grabbed her gun, and burst out the front door. I got up to stop her but sat back down when

I realized I was bleeding. I quickly ran into the bathroom, pulled a shard of glass out of my cheek, pressed a hand towel against the wound, and headed out in search of Zoey..

As I rounded the corner to the backyard, I heard a shot. My heart dropped into the pit of my stomach. I ran in the direction I thought it had come from. I slowed once I entered the woods so that I could tune into sounds. I heard twigs breaking not far to the east. Tentatively, I sang the familiar "whooo-ah" that my friends and I use to identify ourselves when separated out on the trails. I didn't hear a reply.

I could be hit by either Zoey or the shooter if I made too much noise. I stopped to listen. The sounds grew closer, so I tucked behind a tree. Taking a terrible chance, I whooo-ah'd again. She whispered, "Shhhhh, it's me."

"What the fuck were you thinking?" I blurted.

"I'm not going to sit around and be a victim. This is our house. Our god-damned house!" She stomped her foot. "It's supposed to be safe. Look at you." Then she exclaimed. "Oh, my god, you're hurt." She put her hand to my face.

"I'm fine. It was only a piece of glass. I'm sure it's fine. Let's go in and call the police." I looked at Zoey. Her pupils were dilated. She still looked intense. She was scaring me more than the shot had. She slowed her breathing and regained control of her emotions. We were both unsteady as we walked back to the house. After she tended to my cut with butterfly bandages, we waited outside for a squad.

"Who fired the shot out there?" I had to know.

"I saw him running away, and I took a shot. I don't think I hit him, but he got the message. I'm not going to just be a sitting duck." She said it with a calmness that scared me all over again.

"Who are you?" I said.

"I'm who I've always been. This is me trying to cope. We've run away. We've endured protective custody. What else is there? Sit around and wait to be killed? Watch you be killed?" She regained some of the fire in her eyes.

I held her hand in silence until the police arrived. I recognized the federal agents who had talked to me earlier. They secured the house and did a perimeter check of the property. Then they separated us and interviewed us one at a time. When they were through, they cautioned Zoey about going after a would-be gunman on her own. Had she hit him, even though he shot at us, there was a possibility that she would be sued or even investigated criminally unless it happened inside our house. She listened to their advice, still wearing that steely look of resolve on her face.

I offered the agents coffee before grilling them about the shooter. The profiler talked with us while the other two worked at removing the slug embedded in the wall behind the woodstove. It had shattered a ceramic tile and lodged in the cement backer board. They dug around the slug with a common pocketknife and gently pulled it out with a pair of rubber-coated needlenose pliers. The bullet looked smashed to me, but they still handled it gingerly. Vincent said they were tracking down a couple of angles, refusing to be forthcoming about their theories. I got the distinct impression that he wondered if we had manufactured the whole event. I could tell from the set in Zoey's jaw that she had figured that out, too.

When he paused briefly, Zoey told him off. "Look, I know you're working with little information here, but we did *not* make this up. We don't need to be revictimized by you. We called you for help. Why do you think I went out and got a gun? Because the murderer is still out there. This has been going on and on and on." Her voice kept getting louder and going up in pitch.

She pointed at him. "Turn that high-powered brain of yours around and point it in a direction that's going to help us. We've tried to run away from this threat, tolerated protective custody, and yes, today I fought back. I'm not done fighting back. I don't care if I get sued. I'm not going to stand by and be victimized over and over again. I won't tolerate being revictimized by you, either. We're done here." She crossed her arms, widened her stance, and looked him in the eye.

He murmured an apology and left us to rejoin his team. They moved out into the woods, presumably to track down Zoey's slug.

As soon as they were gone, Zoey focused in on me. I could feel her anger as she squared off. I decided to do a pre-emptive strike of my own. "Hon. What's going on with you?"

"I think it's pretty obvious. I'm angry."

"At me?" I took a step back.

"At everything." She softened a bit when she realized I was afraid of her. Not afraid that she'd physically hurt me, but afraid she would lash out emotionally.

"If you weren't looking into other work, I'd be coming at you. Something has to change." Her fists were clenched; her face red. I braced my arms in front of me for support. I didn't quite know how to respond to her like this.

"I'm in survival mode. I'm angry, and I'm expressing my anger. Where the hell is yours? Why aren't you in survival mode, too?" She nearly shouted.

I backed up another step. "Can we take a moment here? Calm down?"

She took several long breaths before continuing. "I'm losing it, aren't I?" She stepped into me, her anger now turning to tears. I held her. I sensed someone watching us and looked up to find Vincent standing just inside the tree line.

"This is private," I told him, while ushering Zoey around the front of the house and into the porch where we sat on the loveseat in silence until I called for the FBI team to rejoin us.

Vincent said that they hadn't found Zoey's slug, as there were too many trees out there to search. They wanted her to retrace her steps as best she could. I could tell that she was exhausted, but she agreed to attempt it. I joined the group, and we re-enacted the chase. She stopped where she thought she had taken the shot. The two investigators fanned out ahead of us, scanning the trees at shoulder height.

Suddenly one of them hollered, "I've got something here." We all walked to where he stood. A few bright red droplets sprinkled the leaves. The officers told us to go home and wait while they followed the blood trail.

When we got back to the house, I removed the broken glass from the window and the shards littering the floor while Zoey processed the fact that she had shot someone. She looked numb, then angry, then numb again. She was an emotional wreck. I had never seen her lose her balance so completely.

I sat her down on the couch and called Donna, who is Zoey's best friend and a nurse practitioner. Donna said she'd be right over. I sat next to Zoey in silence until Donna arrived.

I returned to working on the window. It was a new window with easily removable panes, one that I had previously repaired when a gang member had made an attempt on my life. Zoey had every reason to be angry. I sealed the gaping hole with cardboard, plastic, and duct tape. I stepped back to inspect the ugly wound on our house. It made me wonder how wounded we both were from the recent events. The thought of Zoey losing her composure didn't fit with how I knew her.

"Jo, how are you?" Donna asked.

"Not so good." I shook my head.

"Tell me." She employed a good interviewing technique—open-ended questions.

"We're in danger. Have been repeatedly. The people who are supposed to protect us are suspicious of us. Nothing we do is helping. My girlfriend is losing it. Being accused of murder didn't help. I'm scared. Does that cover it?" She reached over and held my hand.

"This is quite the situation, guys. Now I'm going to say this once, and you're going to do as I say, okay?" We stared at her.

"You're packing up your clothes, dogs, any food that will rot, and moving in with us."

I shook my head no. Zoey agreed with me. "We're not putting two more people in danger. This is bad enough."

"I appreciate the offer, Donna," I said, "but let's wait and see what the FBI wants us to do. This time they found blood out there. We didn't fake that. Nate is due back soon. It's getting dark, so the FBI team will be back shortly. Let's hear what their plan is before making any decisions."

I didn't like dealing with so much turmoil with Zoey and with my friends. I was on thin ice with all of them, but I really didn't want to bring anyone else into this nightmare. Sure, they wanted to be supportive, but did Donna really understand what she was offering?

Zoey shivered, so I built a small fire in the woodstove. The wounded window and gouge behind the stove served as potent reminders that this was no longer our safe haven. The dogs were nowhere in sight. I called for them but got no response. We found them hiding under the dining room table, shaking. We coaxed them out and cuddled them back into some semblance of mental health. We were all losing it.

Full darkness descended, and we caught sight of flashlights peering out from the woods. The agents regrouped in the living room, thankful for the warmth.

"We followed the trail across the river to the south," said the lead investigator. "Whoever it was climbed the bank just before the bridge and must have either had a car waiting or was picked up. We did discover one more critical piece of information. We found two incendiary devices in the woods behind your house. This likely ties the two investigations together."

Before he could go on, Vincent interrupted him and made a heartfelt apology to both of us, saying that he shouldn't have been accusatory.

I felt hopeful that Nate would get to the bottom of things, now that we had proof that the cases were related. Because of the woodsy terrain, it would be impossible for the FBI to protect the house by simply putting a car in our driveway. They wanted to take us into protective custody. They made the same offer of a Super 8 with a guard that Nate had made. It seemed that these professionals were always a step behind the action.

Zoey sighed heavily. She needed to work. How she could work with all of this going on was beyond me. We walked into the house to talk about it. Zoey did not want to stay at the Super 8. She suggested we either move in with Nate or bunk down at Kathy and Donna's. How many times did we have to keep making this decision?

I looked around at our home. It pissed me off that someone had violated the sanctity of our home, our safety, and our relationship. The strain hung between us. I wanted Zoey to have as much input into this as possible.

"I'll do whatever you say." I touched her arm.

"You can't do what I want."

I stayed silent, afraid of making things worse. I went around behind her to massage her neck. She moved away from me. I couldn't remember the last time we had really laughed together, or had sex, for that matter. I let the sadness wash over me.

Chapter 27

As it turned out, after we discussed the options with the FBI agents, they made the decision for us. They wanted to place us at Kathy and Donna's. That way, they could keep their personnel relatively close together in case they needed backup at one location or the other. The DPD had an officer who was roughly my height and weight with short, dark curly hair. He would move into the house and pose as me. Another was assigned to accompany us and stand watch at Kathy and Donna's twenty-acre homestead.

We packed up our clothes, dogs, and all the food we could manage and headed over. Zoey took her car, and I took my new bike. We quickly moved our belongings into the guest room and then updated our friends. Zoey would work from their home as much as possible, and I would begin apprenticing with Kathy on the green kitchen build.

Our dogs seemed more relaxed, choosing their usual comfortable spots and settling in—they were used to spending a lot of time at K&D's. By this time, we all were.

I spent the next morning arranging to have my living room window fixed and shopping for recycled plastic lumber, which Kathy had suggested for the two chairs I would build for my first customer. The plastic would be durable and meet the standards for sustainability that were important in green construction, but somehow working with it didn't feel the same as working with real wood. I enjoyed bringing out the natural grain in wood pieces, especially when refinishing furniture.

While building with new lumber had its joys, refinishing old wood was even more satisfying to me. I liked reclaiming a piece, which often meant deconstructing it; stripping and sanding the old finish off; and filling and repairing damaged places. Bracing and gluing parts of the furniture back together was not unlike my work in probation. We had to lock human beings in cages to take them down to their basic selves and then try to slowly fill in the empty places in their souls and help them return to a life of sobriety and participation in a wholesome community. It wasn't as easy as hanging out with upstanding citizens, but helping an ex-con, ex-drug offender make a new start felt better than anything else I would ever accomplish.

Maybe working with criminals was part of the reason why I wasn't reacting to the stalker in the way Zoey was. Sure, the person was getting to me and causing havoc in my life. But underneath the fear, I held out hope because I'd seen serious criminals turn things around to the point where they held jobs, parented children, and even bought homes. Rehabilitation and restitution were possible, but neither outcome was made more likely with a gun. In fact, guns were deadly, and dead was not the outcome anyone would benefit from, not even someone shooting in self-defense.

That Zoey would want to fight back was natural, but I thought her work with mentally ill clients was similar to the way I worked with juvenile and adult offenders. You couldn't help a psychotic patient with bullets. You could slow him or her down, and you could end a life, but the harm would blow back on you. I had thought that seeing the blood trail in the woods would be enough to quell Zoey's desire to carry a handgun. Apparently, I was wrong.

That evening, we went for a hike along the river trail. Our bodyguard came along. His high-top, combat-style boots were well suited for the task, and he didn't complain.

Storm clouds were gathering in the early evening sky, and I took some comfort knowing that bad guys are usually fair-weather prowlers. Back at the house, I lay in an easy chair and dozed off. Before a dream had any chance of forming in my mind, the ring of my cell phone jerked me awake. Nate was calling to inform us that Diane's funeral would be held the following day at 2 p.m. at the First Lutheran Church of Christ in west Duluth. Nate thought it would be a good idea for us to attend.

Kathy, Donna, and I met Zoey at the church. Undercover police were stationed near every exit and throughout the church. According to Nate, a number of the cops present weren't convinced of my innocence. I felt their glares but brushed them off. Having been accused of the victim's killing made the situation awkward for me at best. I was glad when Nate sat down next to me, his big body forming a bulwark of strength and support.

Diane's family sat in the front row, and a lesbian joined them before the ceremony started.

I leaned into Nate and said, "That might be the girlfriend." I nodded toward the woman seated to the right of Diane's family. She was easily over six foot tall with short blond hair, sitting ramrod straight in the pew.

"How do you know?" he said.

"Are you serious? Have you no gaydar at all?" I nodded toward her again.

"That depends. What is it?"

"Do I have to spell everything out for you? Radar for queers, you big putz." As I said it, the woman in the front row turned and looked at me. She couldn't have heard me, but she must have sensed that I was talking about her because she shot me a glare so deliberate and intense that even Nate reacted.

"Holy shit, Jo, are you sure you don't know her?" he elbowed me.

I returned her gaze without looking away. She turned back and faced the casket. A chill went down my spine. Somewhere my intuition was screaming, *Who is this freak?* Then I remembered. She was the woman I had met at the gym.

When the funeral concluded, she glared at me again as she passed, walking with a slight limp. Nate made a call to one of the Feds, requesting that someone follow her. His description was letter perfect. I made a mental note to have him train me on suspect I.D.

Zoey and I drove our vehicles to K & D's separately, taking an indirect route so that the officer assigned to us could monitor whether we were being followed. I felt drained from the funeral. To be reminded so literally of our vulnerability to a killer and the fatal consequences we might face unnerved me. I couldn't wait to see my dogs and find a way to hold Zoey. That wish was crushed when we got back to the house. Rob, the DPD officer assigned to us, came up to us in a rush.

"We need you to go inside the house right now. All of you. Go to an interior room, turn your cell phone on, and wait." He placed his hand on the small of my back in an effort to guide me. That small condescending act was enough to put me over the edge. It's one of those things men do that absolutely infuriates me.

"Tell me what's going on, or I'm not moving," I said. Zoey gave me a surprised look. She must have been thinking, *Way to go, hon. Way to finally start getting angry.*

He stepped back a little and replied, "Someone's at your house. We want you secure."

I went into the house, followed by Zoey, Kathy, Donna, and the dogs. We chose the family room in the basement as our safest bet and sat there silently waiting. Zoey finally piped up, "I wish I had my gun with me." No one dignified her comment with a response.

She crossed her arms, reflecting a side to Zoey I didn't know existed. Sure, she had stepped up before, in heroic ways even, but the gun thing was new. Even after using the gun and presumably injuring the stalker, she still saw it as a viable way to protect herself and regain her sense of security. Perhaps being with me was changing her. I could tell from Donna's look that she was concerned, too.

Zoey got up and paced. She stopped and sat back down, I walked over to her and tried to rub her neck, but she moved away from me.

After about fifteen minutes, Rob came down and gave us the "all clear."

"What's going on?" I inquired.

"A suspect was questioned and released."

"Who?"

"I'm not at liberty to say."

"Then let me talk to your supervisor." I was angry, and my tone showed it.

"Lieutenant Nathan."

I speed-dialed Nate as we all moved upstairs. He said the woman from the funeral, someone named Camille, had come to my house. When the police questioned her, she said that she only wanted to talk to me about Diane. She was really worked up about me having had an "affair" with Diane. Nate and I were both bothered by the fact that she had driven directly to my house, which is unlisted. He vowed to keep a close eye on her.

Kathy and Donna were a little taken aback by being herded into their house for safekeeping. The danger we were in became a little more real after that. They were more supportive than scared, though, and we started a high-spirited game of hearts to change the mood.

When we climbed into bed, Zoey was curiously quiet. She finally let me touch her, so I massaged her neck and then cradled her in my arms before trailing off to sleep. In the morning, Zoey, red-eyed, sat at the kitchen table.

Kathy got a call indicating that the materials we had ordered for the kitchen project were scheduled for delivery around noon. I hadn't expected to work on the weekend, but Zoey said that she and Donna had research they wanted to catch up on at the university, too. We didn't speak much before she and Donna left.

Kathy brought me out to her shop and taught me how to build cabinet bases. She reasoned that I needed another side business to keep me busy in our new venture, and making custom cabinets would be profitable if we could secure a good price on bamboo lumber. No other cabinetmaker in the area offered bamboo kitchens, but they were popular in other parts of the country in green builds. Custom cabinetry was in high demand for remodeling projects, too, as kitchens in old houses are rarely square. Building a cabinet is really just making a simple box. The secret, she told me, was in providing the customer a nice selection of cabinet doors.

We headed over to the work site, bodyguard in tow, and offloaded the truck. It took most of the afternoon to unpackage the materials, stack the flooring, and finish assembling the cabinets. Kathy and I also double-checked the layout of the kitchen, the outlet placements, and the dimensions of the cabinets against her plans. We found one cabinet that wasn't finished on the outside and we brought it back to the shop to be refaced with birch.

Once back at the house, I played with my dogs while Kathy messed around in the shop. When Kathy came out, she said that the cabinet would have to be exchanged. She didn't have the right sized lumber on hand to customize it. She wanted me to run it into town the next morning as soon as the cabinet store opened. I realized that my apprenticeship put me in a grunt position with Kathy, so I didn't argue.

Chapter 28

THE RUN INTO TOWN WAS UNEVENTFUL, or so I thought. When I came out of the shop, the cop assigned to me approached. "That Camille woman put a tracking device on your car."

My eyebrows went up. It was actually Kathy's car. "So, you took it off, right?"

"No, ma'am. We'd like you to help us set a trap for her."

That got my attention. "What kind of trap?"

"You drive to a secluded place that we can control, and then we see what happens."

"See what happens?"

"Don't worry. We won't lose control. We'll have ten guys on this. She won't stand a chance."

"Why not arrest her for planting the device? Isn't that illegal?" Their track record for catching my stalker had been abysmal to this point, but somehow that thought didn't penetrate my thinking.

"Sure, but it's not a felony. She'd be out of jail in hours. We need to see what she has planned."

"Planting a tracking device is only a misdemeanor?"

"It's not really covered by statute. The law can't keep up with technology. We have to establish that she's stalking you. Stalking implies relentless intent."

I shuddered at the use of the word *relentless*—so apt for the behavior of my stalker. After updating a disagreeable Kathy en route, I followed the cop to a gravel pit outside Lakewood, a small township near the Valley. The ride took about fifteen minutes. Once we were in the gravel pit, the team set up surveillance off to the right of the only entry road in sight. The police contacted the owner, and he cleared out for the morning while the officers took up watch points in his machinery.

I walked around, pretending to look for agates. The police had outfitted me with a bulletproof vest and a wire. I thought about the situation as I strolled the pit, picking up an occasional rock. Anyone who knew me knew that I would never waste time on agate hunting, but what the heck? I needed to see the person I was up against.

Could Camille be the one who took a shot at our house? That didn't make sense. Incendiary devices had been found, and the Jones skinheads were the ones who had torched the houses—unless she had mimicked the arson cases to throw the scent off of her. Obviously she thought I had been having an affair with Diane. But she told the police that she and Diane had broken up. Did she blame me for that? What if she was the one who had been stalking me from the beginning?

Lost in thought, I barely registered that a car had pulled up. The woman from the funeral I now knew to be Camille charged out at me. I fisted a large rock as she approached. "Stop right there."

She pulled up short. "You had no right."

"No right to do what?"

"To go to her funeral." She spat the words.

"Whoa! Who are you?"

"Diane's partner—or I was. I'm the one she left for you." Her fists were clenched. At least they were where I could see them. "I'm the one who loved her."

"I don't doubt that. Look, I don't know what you thought happened, but there wasn't anything between Diane and me. Not for at least ten years, anyway."

"You liar!" she hissed. "I have proof." Red blotches were appearing on her neck. I could smell a musky sweet smell.

"You can't have proof of something that didn't happen," I said calmly. I didn't want this to get physical. She was a freaking Amazon. At six foot, she was taller than I, and she appeared to spend a lot of time in the weight room.

"Here!" She reached into her pocket, sending my heart into a fast cadence. When her hand emerged, she was holding a picture. I relaxed. My stomach quivered as I reached for the picture. Then I stepped back, placing some distance between us again.

It was a picture of me kissing Zoey in our living room. We were dancing, and her hand was under my shirt on my back.

"This is me and my partner."

"She wasn't your fucking partner!" she screamed.

"My partner, Zoey. This is our home. This is me and Zoey." I remembered that Diane resembled Zoey in size, weight, and even hair color. "Look at the hair closer. Zoey's is curlier. These are her clothes. This is Zoey," I repeated. "How did you get this?" I knew the answer to the question. She had taken the picture herself from behind our house. She was the voyeur.

"You took this while you were spying on us," I said, getting angry when she wouldn't respond. She just kept giving me that intense look of pure hate.

Finally she spoke. "No, this is you and Diane. She was always gone. 'Where were you?' I'd ask. You know what she'd say to me? 'I was with Jo.' She never got over you. You were never really apart. But you didn't love her like I did. No one did. Now she's gone."

She reached behind her, and I rushed her and knocked her to the ground. Everything happened in slow motion. My legs felt heavy as I got up and ran toward the area where I thought the police would be waiting to ambush the suspect.

When we heard the sound of a car approaching the opening to the pit, Camille stopped pursuing me and dashed for her car. I kept running in the opposite direction. Vest or no vest, I wasn't going to mess around.

Cops materialized from the rim of the pit, yelling commands to freeze. She started her car and floored it, sending gravel flying. One officer hazarded a shot, presumably at Camille's tires, but she gained traction and shot out of the pit just as another car entered. She sideswiped the squad and kept going. The driver screamed into the radio as he turned a painfully slow U-turn in the pit. I heard the wail of sirens as I made my way to Kathy's car, which thankfully wasn't damaged.

Purely by chance, neither was I. So much for the big trap in a place where the police could maintain control. I pulled off the vest and wire, ripped the tracking device off, and drove home without another word. Furious with the police for fucking up their operation so badly, I sat in the car for a few minutes, trying to center myself before joining Kathy at the work site.

That evening in bed, I told Zoey everything. I needed to understand what was going on psychologically with Camille. After her initial shock, Zoey made me promise not to pull a stunt like that again. Then she agreed with me that Camille had to be the photographer from the woods. Based on what I told her about Camille, Zoey couldn't determine whether she was capable of killing Diane, let alone cutting off her hand.

"Which hand was severed, I wonder," she said, thinking out loud. "If Diane had worn a ring, the hand could signify a broken commitment."

She warned me that a person capable of cutting off another person's hand either had serious mental health problems or was a cold-blooded killer.

Chapter 29

KATHY AND I LEFT AT 7:30 the next morning. She was angry with me for pulling the stunt in the gravel pit. She could get in line to express her anger as far as I was concerned. Everyone was angry with me. I was angry with the police for screwing it up.

On the way to the work site, I called my boss. The ethics committee was scheduled to meet Friday to discuss my situation. Chief Knight assured me he had no doubt I'd be cleared to return to work soon, but the board had the final say. The board, made up of County Commissioners, is political as hell. They would review the findings of the committee and be advised by the agency lawyer before making a decision. Slowing down the process further, the board didn't meet until the last Friday of the month. That left me at least three weeks off, enough time to try out the idea of working with Kathy. I might even consider extending my leave if I wanted to give the carpentry option a longer trial.

My relationship with Zoey was on the line, and I wasn't prepared to lose it. She was the best thing that had ever happened to me. I was growing as a person because I was taking risks with her I didn't even know I had been avoiding. Deep down, I knew that I would never find out who I was really capable of being without her in my life. I prayed that she wasn't tiring of the endless threats. I knew our bond was solid, and I was counting on it to help us get through this. There had to be an end to the madness sometime, didn't there?

On a work break, I called Nate to see if the police had caught Camille. He was glad to hear from me, and embarrassed and apologetic about how the PD had botched the trap. He assured me that if he had been there, Camille would be in custody right now. As it stood, she was still at large. An "attempt to locate" warrant had been issued, and once found, she would be charged with several felonies, including assault on a police officer, criminal vehicular damage, and the charges associated with stalking me.

The work on the kitchen came along nicely. We hung cabinets, and they looked great. The light birch-maple combination made the kitchen look bright and clean. Kathy and I took final measurements for the countertop, and she did a hand rendering on the spot to fax the manufacturer when we got home. It felt good to stand back at the end of the day and look at what we had accomplished. Kathy's eye for details amazed me, and I felt lucky to be learning from her. This also fit well with my own tendencies toward perfectionism.

Focusing on the carpentry had actually allowed me to tune out the mess the rest of my life was in. Thankfully, Kathy didn't have a need to process it with me. The presence of the guard was a constant reminder, though, of the protection I needed. Keeping him on duty must have been costing the DPD dearly, and the investment they were making almost made me forgive them the debacle at the gravel pit. Almost.

We got home before Zoey and Donna, so Kathy and I took all four dogs on a long walk to my house on the outer loop trail. I called Nate and asked him to alert our "house guest." I wondered how the officer liked his digs. The thought of a man peeing in our bathroom and sleeping in our bed didn't sit well with me. When we arrived, I kenneled the dogs and rang my own bell.

A man, dressed in a comfortable cardigan sweater, opened the door and welcomed us in. Maybe the PD did have some gay men on the force after all. The smell of coffee overwhelmed me as I entered, and he offered us homemade scones and frothed-up lattés as we sat at the kitchen island. It felt weird and comforting at the same time to be served in my own house. I was thankful the guy seemed to be thoroughly enjoying his assignment. The place looked clean and well cared for. He was keeping a list of all the movies he had ordered on the satellite dish and would leave cash to cover the costs. He didn't offer any updates on Camille, but he said that five men had been arrested in the arson cases, including Curtis Jones. The national white supremacy organization denied any ties to the local skinhead gang and denounced the harm done to any fine upstanding white community members.

I hoped that the rift between the Jones gang and the national organization would mean that the persons arrested couldn't make bail, and would be dependent on public defenders to fight the charges. Since a judge and police chief had been targeted, those accused would receive no leniency from judge or jury.

By the time we finished our coffee and scones, it was getting dark. I called Zoey, and she came to pick us up. I sat in the backseat with four dogs. The dogs licked and snuggled me until I felt raw. Kathy and Zoey laughed and encouraged them the whole way home.

At dinner, Zoey and Donna grilled me on how the building project was going, and being honest, I told them I found it quite rewarding. I didn't tell them that I missed my staff—even some of the clients—and the familiar collegiality of our office.

"I'll be on paid leave for at least three more weeks," I told them.

When I shared that I had made an initial inquiry about taking a leave of absence, they all looked pleased. I'd been toying around in my mind with the idea of taking a year off to let things settle down. I was sure that the danger my work had put us in was a fluke, and with time, things would go back to normal.

Zoey rubbed her toe up and down my leg under the table, and when I looked over at her, her beauty and nearness combined with an expression that sunk into the depths of my being. I knew that look. It meant *I want you so much I could devour you right here.* I must have stopped talking because Kathy and Donna were looking at us. Finally, Kathy cleared her throat and said, "Why don't you let us clean up tonight, guys? We could use some time alone."

I didn't even look at her, keeping my eyes glued on Zoey. "Thanks, we've got things to talk about, too." I made a slight nod toward the guest room, and Zoey flashed me a sly grin.

We had a difficult time being quiet and ended up with about twenty minutes of laughter for foreplay and a couple of minutes of lovemaking. It was almost like being at one of our parents' houses and making out behind closed doors.

The next morning, Kathy refrained from asking me about our antics, but I could tell she was pleased that we were getting along. She commented on how glad she was that I was thinking about going into business with her. At work, we adjusted the cabinet doors and then laid down the bamboo flooring. Kathy explained that once I started making the cabinets, customers could choose matching floors and cabinets. That would allow her to suggest contrasting countertop designs.

I cautioned her that I wasn't a cabinetmaker yet, but she assured me that I'd catch on after doing a few. We'd start with one style of cabinet doors, and I could learn more as time went on. The floor went in easily, and we finished up early for the day.

Kathy called the homeowner and asked him if he wanted her to do the trim in the kitchen around the door and windows or if he wanted it all done when the rest of the house was finished out. He asked her to do it so that the finishing carpenter could follow her style. She had big plans for crown molding to top off the cabinets in the kitchen and energy efficient lighting under the upper cabinets. Kathy was giddy with the prospect of finishing the kitchen.

When we got home, I wandered around the yard and placed a call to Nate. He actually sounded like he missed me. He also sounded happy about the progress they had made in the firebombing case, adding that he would in all likelihood be up for a promotion soon. I knew he must be tired, but his upbeat attitude was infectious. He invited me out to dinner and asked me to bring Zoey. He was determined to settle the Camille problem as soon as possible. Hoping his undivided attention on my stalker would lead to a quick resolution raised my spirits, too.

The next day, Kathy and I completed the work on the kitchen trim. Now all that was left to do was to install the countertops and appliances. We met the homeowner at a bargain appliance store in Superior, Wisconsin, the other half of the Twin Ports, in early afternoon, and he picked out a top-name-brand stainless fridge, dishwasher, and a gas double oven. Kathy made sure they would fit the openings we had created for them, and arranged for delivery the following day.

When we were through, she dropped me at The Lift, a restaurant that overlooks the lift bridge in Canal Park at the entrance to Duluth's inner bay. I planned to ride home with Zoey. I had an hour to kill, so I did some shopping at an outdoors store. Zoey met me at the front of the restaurant, and we walked in together. Nate was twenty minutes late, but he had already called in his order. Zoey and I split a plate of fettuccini Alfredo and Tuscan red wine linguini. Nate's order of pesto pasta with scallops was served right before he strolled in. I vowed to remember his trick.

He plopped down and immediately dug into his food.

"Hey, guys, I freaking love this place. Doesn't the smell make you ravenous?" He took a big bite.

"The food is really good. Any luck tracking down Camille?"

"Not a bit. We got a warrant and searched her apartment. Other than her being a clean freak, nothing stood out."

"What does she do for work?"

"The woman is independently wealthy. She gets a stipend from a trust she inherited from the sale of her parents' business. It's enough so she doesn't have to work if she doesn't want to."

"Can you track her spending?"

"Not on this kind of a case. It takes a lot to invade someone's life that much. We asked for it, but the prosecutor declined, saying it isn't normal in cases like this. You know, could be construed as discrimination because of the charges against our officers." He took a fist-sized bite of his pasta. The guy knew his way around a plate.

"Did you check Diane's place?" Zoey inquired.

"Holy shit, Zoey, that's right. No, we haven't, but I'm going to. Didn't even think of that. See, this dinner with you is already paying off. Ever think about being a profiler?"

"No, thanks. I'm trying to get us out of the crook business," Zoey answered, and I grimaced a bit.

"What else can you add, Zoey? I'm curious about how Camille's mind works."

I jumped in, "I might have a lead for you." Nate raised his eyebrows. "Check the health clubs and gyms. The woman has to be working out. I can tell you that right now. I saw her at my gym once, and she is a weight-lifting junkie."

"Which gym?"

"Tech Fit. My staff got me to sign up over there."

"Another excellent idea. I'll look into it. I doubt she has stayed with the same gym, but if she switched, maybe we can find a receipt in her belongings." Nate kept eating.

"Did you find any camouflage gear in her apartment? The person in our woods had camo. gear."

"No such luck."

"Photography gear?"

"We found a camera bag, and we're searching the contents of her computer. If she has pictures of you, we'll find them. That would definitely tie her in, but I'm not sure that would be enough to charge her with attempted murder."

"She walked with a limp at the funeral. What are the chances she's the one I shot?" Zoey didn't eat, focusing instead on the conversation.

"Well, we did think of that. We won't know until we find her, and even then, unless we have the slug and can match it to your gun, a wound won't mean much."

"Shit." I needed to vent some frustration.

"Tell me about Diane's hand. The one you found on our property," Zoey probed.

Nate took a minute, scratching his head with one big, beefy paw. His black eyes were totally healed now, but he still looked like a shaggy street dog.

"I'm not sure I can release that much to you."

"Nate, how can I help you if you won't give me something to work with? I really think the hand is significant," Zoey said.

"Tell me more. I'm interested in your theory about that."

Zoey nodded. "Okay, first off, if it was her left hand, it might symbolize a broken commitment. She believed Jo came between them. Delivering the hand to Jo, and then having it be used against her to frame her would be some kind of justice in her mind. If the hand had a ring on it, I'd try to determine if Diane had ever worn the ring, or if it was placed on the hand postmortem to deliver a message."

"Interesting, keep going." Nate closed in on the last bite of his food.

"That's all I have. It's pretty obvious."

"Hang on, I have a question," I said. "Did the police find any evidence of an incendiary device at Camille's place?" I also barely ate. This was important.

"Not a thing." He shook his head slowly no.

We hadn't learned anything new. But maybe we had given Nate something to work with. I was counting on him to catch up with Camille before she caught up with us. As we parted for the night, Nate pulled me aside and told me that Lou had asked him to say, "Hi, and hurry back."

Chapter 30

WE SLEPT IN ON SATURDAY and took the short drive to the Lakeview Castle for breakfast. I wasn't used to going out to eat so much, but I figured the extra labor in my new job would make up for some of my indulgences. The breakfast buffet was fantastic, and we all overate. I treated Kathy and Donna as small thanks for putting us up. We then went grocery shopping in Two Harbors.

When we got home, Kathy asked if we wanted to help out on a project she had in mind. She planned to build a bridge on her property over a small swampy area. Of course, given Kathy's vocation, it wasn't small, or simple. The bridge turned out to be twenty feet long, a boardwalk of sorts with a decorative arbor in the middle. With all four of us working on it, we got the bridge partially done in one day. It occurred to me that choosing carpentry as my day job would make these weekend construction projects at home less fun as time went on. The idea made me feel slightly disoriented.

I also found myself wondering about Brian. Maybe he would enjoy helping out with a few odd jobs in the Valley. It would give him a little extra cash and a template for what an honest life might look like.

We walked the dogs late in the afternoon, enjoyed a relaxing sauna, and then fell into bed exhausted. Kathy and I finished the arbor on Sunday while Donna and Zoey went into town to browse rummage sales. It was fun to hang so closely with our best friends, but I worried we were overstaying our welcome. I wanted Camille locked up and out of our lives.

On Sunday night, I broke down and called Nate. The police had searched Diane's place and found evidence that Camille had stayed there. She destroyed a couple of the pictures of me by burning them. I cringed a bit after hearing about the use of fire. Nate continued the extra security at my house and even took a shift on his own. They had a near miss in capturing her at her gym. She made the police and bolted before getting out of her car. Nate had a bad feeling about what she planned to do next, and cautioned me to beware. He asked me to spend more time talking things over with Zoey and to call him back if we came up with something new.

In the morning, I told Kathy that I needed some time away from the kitchen project. She grilled me about what I was going to do. I told her I wanted to take a long ride to clear my head and sort things out. Kathy offered to follow me in her car. I thanked her for the offer but said I needed space.

Somewhere I had read that motorcyclists and plane pilots can lower their blood pressure simply by driving and flying because, having to focus on so many things at once, their minds let go of other stressors. It always seemed to work for me.

I headed through Duluth and over into Superior, following the south shore of the lake. Sun shone through a cloudless blue sky. With one eye on my rearview mirror to make sure I wasn't being followed, I sorted through the direction I wanted my life to take.

I really love my job, and ordinarily it's safer than a traditional PO job. As a supervisor, I have much less direct contact with clients. Sitting at that damn desk, though, is a royal pain. The paperwork is monotonous. If I didn't drink a lot of coffee, I'd go batty. Helping my PO's do surveillance and arrests on occasion always perks things up.

Perhaps I'm deluding myself, thinking that I'd be content to remodel and build kitchens. Where would be the excitement in that? Could I let go of helping wayward kids?

Riding my cycle and scanning the horizon, I realized that even this pastime was a risky one. And yet I chose it to clear my head. Could I really trade the sometimes exciting life of a probation officer for a job remodeling and building kitchens? Maybe my need to ride a cycle was part and parcel of some warped need for speed, and adrenaline.

What in the hell does Zoey see in me? I'm going to get us both killed. Shit! Even if we survive, will our relationship? What about my relationship with Kathy and Donna?

By the time I reached Bayfield, I hadn't made any more progress in my thinking. In an attempt to turn my thoughts in a more positive direction, I stopped at a diner and picked up a sandwich and then set off on foot to explore the Myers Beach Sea Caves trail.

It was a beautiful day, and the lake was calm. When I got to the scenic overlook with a view of one of the caves, I worked my way down to the jagged shoreline and found a spot in the sun that was relatively sheltered from the wind. I was certain no one could see me.

I ate my sandwich, took my shirt off, and basked in the sun. Then I called Zoey.

"Hey, hon. I'm glad I caught you at your desk."

Zoey's reply had a sense of urgency that made me sad. "Everything okay?"

"Sure. I didn't mean to scare you. I'm on the south shore, looking out at the Apostle Islands with my shirt off in the sun."

"Nice!"

"Wish you were here."

"Me too, actually. I'm finding it impossible to focus today." She had a slight whine to her voice.

"My thoughts are a little black myself. I wish this would all end. I miss our life."

"Me, too," she replied. "I want to get your old bike out of jail and be there riding right next to you."

My heart soared. We had a chance.

"When is your next break?"

"Summer."

"Like in June?"

"The second of June."

"Let's come back here."

"Promise?"

"Promise."

I felt the weight of that promise. I wanted so much to be there for Zoey. No matter what happened with my job or what Camille tried to do, I needed her. She was the one constant in my life I could count on. I needed to tell her that. I promised myself I'd share more with her.

I cleared my mind for the ride home, and actually enjoyed the sights, smells, and curves of the winding, scenic road.

On Tuesday, Kathy and I got back to work on the kitchen. The appliances were in, and we were meeting the plumber to team up on the installation. There was also a chance that the countertops would be ready in the afternoon.

We hooked up the trailer, loaded up my Adirondack rockers, and headed off to work. Finally the kitchen install was complete. When we got home, the homeowner called to say how much he loved the kitchen and the Adirondacks. Kathy handed me the phone so that I could hear him thank me personally. It felt odd to have someone thank me for doing work for him. In the probation business, that rarely happened. I wondered if I could actually make the transition. I looked down at my big hands. Maybe this was what I was meant to do with my life.

I planned to sit down with Kathy and go over the financial possibilities, imagining that making pay similar to the salary and benefits of my Probation Supervisor job would be improbable. Not to mention the retirement package and deferred compensation account I was building. It was a lot to give up. I could retire at age fifty-seven if I stayed on my current career path. I doubted I could do that as a contractor's helper.

After we finished work for the day, I took off for another ride. I headed into Duluth and then wandered toward Highway 23, a newly paved roadway that winds its way along the St. Louis River from the far west end of Duluth through a state park, ending in Cloquet, Minnesota. The road is a favorite of cyclists because of its curves and scenic overlooks.

I don't often allow myself pure pleasure rides, but each time I take one, I vow to take more. The vibration from my bike turned into an internal purring, and I could feel a happiness and contentment that radiated from inside me.

Halfway through the ride, I started feeling a little guilty. While I was enjoying the ride, I couldn't help wondering what was going on with Brian.

I pulled over to a scenic overlook and called Karen at the office. She had been meeting with Brian daily and would know by now if they had established a strong enough rapport for her to help him. She didn't answer, so I called her cell. She picked up after four rings. I got off my bike and walked down by the river to sit on a log.

"Hey, Karen, it's Jo Spence."

"Jo, how are you?"

"I'm good. I'm taking a break from a fantastic cycle ride."

"Nice! And getting paid for it, too."

"Yup." I smiled. "How is Brian?

"He's great. I can see why you're so attached to him."

"So, he's talking to you?"

"Absolutely. It took awhile. He was pretty broken up that you were out of the picture, but we're connecting well now. I can't get over how normal he is with that man for a father!" Anger seeped through the phone.

"I know," I responded. "Maybe the mom has had a positive influence on him."

"Definitely. How the hell has she stayed with that asshole this long? It's beyond me. Brian's helped himself by seeking out positive role models where he can find them. He has a favorite teacher at school who's mentored him some, and he hangs out at the local rec. center."

"That explains a lot. I was wondering how he could be so warm-hearted, coming from that home."

"He's a survivor for sure," she said.

"Will you say hi to him for me?"

"Absolutely! I'm sure he'll be happy to hear you haven't forgotten about him."

I felt a pang of guilt. I had all but abandoned him. I chose my own safety over his. Trying to hide my emotional response, I asked Karen if she had seen him yet today. He was due in any minute. I asked her if she could bring him to the Rose Garden to meet with me. She agreed to smuggle him out, and I turned my bike back toward Duluth.

When they got out of the car, Brian's face broke into a big smile as soon as he saw me. I could tell he was fighting the urge to run up to me. That was one of the things about him I loved. His youthful innocence. It was rare in a twelve-year-old delinquent. They were usually so guarded. We sat down on a bench and caught up for awhile, talking about his life. Then I told him I wanted him to know that I had to take some time off of work, but that I still cared about him. He looked a little self-conscious, so I fist-bumped him and let him go on his way.

I sat down by the big lake for a few minutes, trying to center myself. I felt the tug of what keeps me motivated at work; the hope of turning some of the kids around by grabbing on to the good in them and nurturing it. It really doesn't take much. Helping kids find themselves and begin down a path of a healthy, happy life was more rewarding than any building project could ever be. In that instant, I knew that I would regret leaving my job permanently. I also knew that if I didn't, it would be a barrier for Zoey and me to overcome. This was an impossible decision.

As soon as I walked in the door, Zoey sensed that something was wrong and pulled me into an embrace. "Mmm, babe, are you okay?"

I told her about seeing Brian and about why my work mattered so much to me. She listened, and I could tell she was saddened by my ambivalence. She really had her hopes up that I would leave my job.

She must have said something to Donna because after dinner Donna went into her study, retrieved a kit of some sort, and called me over to the table. She placed a blood pressure cuff on my arm and took a reading. I didn't like where this was heading.

"What is your blood pressure normally?" she asked.

"I don't know. Falls in the pre-hypertension range."

"Well, it's high now," she said. "You need to see your doctor. Get on some meds."

"Hey, back off here. I'm weighing things, okay?"

"I just want you to have all the facts. I'm a nurse, and this is an important factor. Didn't your mom die of heart disease?"

"Point taken." I had to concede. "I'll make an appointment tomorrow."

I held Zoey all night. I felt the weight of my internal debate about what mattered most in my life and wondered how I could possibly have it all. I felt like I was being torn in half.

Kathy and I spent the following day in her shop. She taught me how to make flat-panel and raised-panel cabinet doors. We constructed a couple of simple pine cabinets for her basement laundry room. We also sat down and went over the details of how much I could earn working with her. Her plan was that I'd get a contractor's license and be the primary contractor on the kitchen projects. On kitchens where the homeowner bought factory cabinets, we'd net around $10,000 ($5,000 each) for an entire kitchen, depending on what kind of contractor's rate we got on the materials. On the custom-made cabinet kitchens, I'd net $7,000. If we did twelve full kitchens a year, I would net roughly $72,000. I could fill in the schedule by building the Adirondack rockers or other custom furniture. Gaps in the kitchen schedule would give Kathy more time to plan and design houses as well. The figures definitely gave me something to think about. A one-year leave of absence to try it out was beginning to sound like a viable option.

Inside though, I felt like I was selling out. Maybe taking a year off would give us enough distance from recent events so that Zoey would see that this stalking ordeal was an anomaly. I could go back to my job, and we could still have a normal, happy, and healthy life together.

Kathy spent the next day developing building plans, and I puttered around cleaning their house. At around noon, I got a call from Zoey. She sounded tense.

"I got an interesting visitor today."

"Who?"

"Camille."

"What happened? Are you all right?"

"I'm fine. She was waiting for me at my office after my eleven o'clock class. She walked up and stared at me. Didn't say a word."

"Are you sure it was her? I mean, have you seen her before?"

"Well, let's see, six feet tall, blond, built like an Amazon? I remember that description."

"Did you call the police?"

"Right before I called you. I'm sure she's long gone now."

"What do you think she wanted?"

"Either she was trying to intimidate me, get a message to you, or see how much I look like Diane. Maybe all three."

"Shit, Zoey. Are you coming home?"

"No, the damage is done. I'm spooked, but I'll work through it."

"Call me later, okay?" I needed some reassurance that she was fine. I wanted to be there, protecting her. I felt both helpless and angry. So much for our future serene life together.

I continued my cleaning, took the dogs for a long walk, and then I received another cell phone call. This time it was from Kelly, the Lieutenant from the Minnesota Gang Strike Force. She wanted me to meet her at my house.

I sped over on the Silverwing. When I got there, I noticed yellow crime scene tape placed over the door to my screen porch. Kelly stood there, looking at me with crossed arms from the porch, dressed in full uniform. I approached slowly.

Car doors slammed, and two more women responded. It barely registered with me how unusual that was. I waited until Margaret Martin, the County Attorney, and Candace Redland, a homicide detective, reached us. Then I shook everyone's hands.

"Looks like I got the A team."

Kelly's face opened up a little at that, and Candace said, "This is strange. We're usually surrounded by men. What are the chances?"

"I still don't know what's going on here," I said casually, "but I know whatever it is, we're well prepared." No one responded.

Candace broke the silence, and pointing toward the crime scene area, looked me in the eye and said, "This is serious, Jo. The officer who was staked out at your house as a decoy is dead. He was cooking in the kitchen and was shot from behind."

I felt a rush of adrenaline punch through my shock. I fought the absurd desire to laugh. It was all too much. "He's dead?"

She nodded slowly. "That was supposed to be you."

"I liked him. He loved our house so much. He called this the best assignment he'd ever had." I pictured him in the kitchen whipping up a batch of scones. "Let me see him."

Candace walked in with me, leaned over a shrouded body, and slowly pulled back the sheet, revealing a head that could have been mine with an exit wound right through the forehead. I bent over and felt instantly nauseous. Margaret guided me over to the sink, where I threw up.

Once I steadied myself, we both went out onto the porch. I lowered myself into one of my rockers. Margaret sat in the other one, looking almost as pale as I felt. We sat there in silence as Candace continued to examine the house for evidence. A coroner's minivan pulled up, and Ann Myers stepped out. I couldn't bring myself to laugh at the irony of yet another woman responding to the crime scene.

The knowledge that the killer had probably been Camille and that she had left here to go directly to Zoey's office penetrated my numb senses. Bile and panic rose in my throat, and I almost lost it a second time.

Back at her house, Kathy gave me some space and made coffee. I kept picturing Randy lying on my kitchen floor. *Would my house ever feel the same? That wonderful man was trying to protect us, and then he was lying on my kitchen floor dead. Did Camille know it wasn't me? He was roughly my height and weight, with curly hair—from behind she could have mistaken him for me. Would she have walked up to the body to make sure she had killed me? I bet she would. Am I safe now? What about Zoey, Kathy, Donna,…my dogs? What the hell had she been doing at Zoey's workplace?* I felt drained.

Then something inside me came alive; a small ball of anger, but I felt it building. I moved from feeling that someone else had to stop Camille to knowing that I would have to do it. I couldn't trust anyone else. They'd let me down time and time again. Even Nate had failed to contain the threat that she posed to me and to Zoey. My anger sparked an energy to fight back, and I would fuel that flame until I could do what I had to do. I got up and paced…thinking.

Zoey had every right to be pissed at me. I had failed as a lover when I let Diane intrude into our lives. And then Camille had followed in Diane's wake. A monster. A murderer.

How can I find her? She wants me. I have to draw her to me somehow. Not here. I can't risk everyone else. No, it has to be me alone. How can I do this without letting Zoey know? She would insist on helping. She and I have gone through threats together before. I know I can trust her. But can I risk her? I knew the answer.

Chapter 31

I SLIPPED QUIETLY OUT of Kathy and Donna's house and then quickly fired up my bike. I prayed I wouldn't pass Zoey's car on my way out. When I got to the road, I turned right and weaved my way into town, using back roads. My cell phone kept vibrating on my hip. I ignored it. This was about me, and I wasn't going to place Zoey in danger anymore.

I drove first to Diane's place, cutting into the alley behind her apartment, checking for police surveillance. Even without that, it wouldn't be easy to enter her central hillside apartment building without neighbors noticing. I killed the engine and parked the bike a half block from the rear of the building, tucking it behind a garage. I crept up to the brick structure and walked the length of it, from back to front, treading quietly close to the wall. Once I reached the front, I reversed my route and moved over to the opposite side, looking out toward the street.

No squads or vans were visible, so I came around to the front and quickly entered the building. I climbed up the stairs to Diane's third-floor apartment. Each step creaked. My heart pounded, but I kept going. My fear fueled the fire inside me, as I pictured Randy on my kitchen floor with a bullet hole in his head.

My phone vibrated again. I looked at the caller I.D. It was Nate.

While I could trust Nate, I didn't want any interference. This was my job to do, and I was going to do it. For a brief moment, I felt apprehension about confronting an armed madwoman with nothing but my anger, but I kept creeping up the stairs.

When I reached the landing on the third floor, I stopped to listen. The old building smelled of pine cleaner and hundred-year-old dust. Somewhere a television set blared an old western. The sound of gunshots made me jump.

As I got closer to Diane's apartment door, I saw that it was blocked off by crime scene tape. Stopping at the door to listen, I heard nothing. When I tried the door handle, it turned. I slowly opened the door and listened again. Still no sound came from inside the apartment.

I ducked under the tape and into the apartment's small living room. Once inside, I stood still and listened again. Sensing that the apartment was empty, I worked my way from room to room, finding nothing until I came to Diane's bedroom.

I was everywhere. Pictures of me dotted a full wall. I stood there in awe of what must have been some kind of sick, twisted fixation. Newspaper articles, high school yearbook photos, photos of her and me when we dated ten years ago. It was all so sad.

The vibration of my phone again brought me back to reality. I silenced the vibration and made my way back out to my bike. I didn't know Camille's address, so I started driving to all of the gyms in town. A fitness freak would turn to her addiction to cope. And that's where I'd hunt her down.

I craved a cup of coffee like nobody's business, but I ignored the temptation. I looked at several gyms before striking gold. Camille was pressing 140 pounds when I found her at the Tone Right Gym in the back room. I stopped her lift midway. She struggled to hold the weight bar in place, and I took some pleasure in that. We were alone in the room. I placed both hands on the bar and lowered it, pinning her to the table. Then I leaned my weight on the bar and removed one hand to speed dial Nate.

"I have her, Nate. Get here. Tone Right Gym on Superior Street, downtown."

"Are you all right?" He rushed his words.

"I am, but she might not be for long. Get here." I disconnected the phone.

Another bodybuilder came in, and I motioned for him to leave. "This is private. The police are on their way."

Camille had trouble breathing with the weight of the bar on her chest, but she did manage to scream, "I'm being assaulted here. Help me."

I held out my phone. "Call 911 if you want to. I just called the cops. She's wanted for murder." The guy simply backed out of the room.

"Get the fuck off me, you bitch," she said through clenched teeth. Her face turned red, and I wondered if I was doing permanent damage. She relaxed to take a breath, and I was starting to think she had passed out. Suddenly she pushed up on the bar with a mighty heave and twisted out from under it. She faced me with the weight bench between us. Sirens blared.

She lunged at me, and I ducked right. I got into my karate stance and prepared for the fight of my life. She seemed huge. She took another swing at me, and I deflected it, throwing her into the far wall by the door. The sirens were getting closer.

"You are so going to die," she said, before running for the door with me right at her heels. She grabbed her bag on the way out and made a quick sprint for a green Subaru Forester.

I followed her on my bike, trailing from a one-block distance. When she stopped at a light before the freeway entrance, I pulled over and tucked in behind a parked car. I pulled out my phone and dialed Nate, updating him on my location.

A gunshot slammed into the fairing on my bike. *Holy shit, that was close.* A foot more and I would have been hit in the chest. I quickly stowed my phone and gunned my throttle, steering straight for Camille's tailgate.

The light changed, and squads were pulling up, but I couldn't afford to wait for someone else.

This is my deal, and I'm not done. I was nearly blind with rage. The thought that she might go after Zoey again made the blood pound in my ears. A voice in my head said, *I'm not letting her escape again.... I'm going to stop her even if it kills me.*

I wanted to run my bike right into her, but I had a shred of sanity left. I didn't know if she sensed my determination or if the sirens pushed her, but she floored the little wagon and took off.

Something inside me made me realize that I was out of control. The voice in my head sounded like the voice in my dream, the one telling me to kill myself in multiple ways. I pictured Zoey in the dream, bending over in anguish at the sound of the voice. She would be hurt if I died. I wouldn't be protecting Zoey by letting my anger lead me into a death battle. I would be forcing her to face a life of grief that would never go away.

Camille had a gun, and I had nothing. I got off my bike, and as the squads caught up to me, I pointed in the direction she had gone. Then I waited for Nate. He escorted me home to face Zoey's wrath. My whole body trembled. I was crashing hard. I just wanted to sleep.

Unexpectedly, Zoey seemed to understand how I had come unglued. She listened to me, encouraged me for not continuing the chase, and lectured me for trying to do it alone. I didn't even have the energy to argue with her. I didn't want to think about what had almost happened. I simply wanted to go to bed.

The next morning, I puttered around in Kathy's shop, working on cabinet designs in between dog walks. At around three, I got a call on my cell. The caller I.D. read "unknown caller." I picked up.

"Jo Spence."

"I have Brian," said a female voice. It sounded like Camille.

My heart fluttered as adrenaline flushed into my body. "Where are you?" I tried to sound calm.

"We're at the Rose Garden. Be here in twenty minutes, or he dies."

"Let me talk to him. I don't believe you."

She simply hung up. She knew she had me.

I ran out to my bike and sped into town. I parked at the far end of the Rose Garden parking lot and entered the park from close to the lake in an attempt to have some control over what was happening. I couldn't let her hurt Brian. Approaching the area from the south, I debated calling Nate. I hit speed dial, but then decided not to place the call, at least not yet. I couldn't risk the police showing up and endangering Brian. I closed my phone.

She wanted me. I wanted Brian safe. Nate would not allow that exchange to take place. I was on my own.

Chapter 32

I CREPT UP FROM THE LAKE WALK, ducking behind rose bushes and benches whenever possible. I couldn't see Camille or Brian, so I climbed up on top of the fountain in the center of the garden to see if I could catch a glimpse of them. Up ahead and to the left, I spotted Camille sitting on a bench beyond a small stand of spruce trees. Brian sat next to her, fidgeting and looking around. He caught sight of me, and bringing my index finger to my mouth, I signaled him to be quiet.

The poor kid had been through a lot in his young life. First, he was a pawn in his dad's stolen bike ring, and more than likely, he had been forced to witness the skinhead attacks on prominent members of the court system. Now, he was being used as a pawn to get to me.

I had no time to formulate a plan. There was a public bathroom just behind the bench where Camille was holding Brian hostage. I decided that I would come from behind the bathroom and try to catch her off guard. Quickly jumping down from the fountain, I made my way back toward the lake so that I could come up behind them. When I was halfway to the structure, my phone rang. I opened it, hoping that Camille had not heard the annoying ringtone.

"Where are you?" she said. "You're running out of time."

"I'm almost there. Is Brian with you?" I wanted her to think I didn't know. I rounded the back of the bathroom.

"You have two minutes, or he dies." She hung up.

He dies echoed through my brain.

I came around the building and didn't stop. I couldn't think about this too much. As I approached, I replaced *he dies* with *he lives*. I was jittery from adrenaline. My legs felt numb, but somehow I kept going. I noticed she wasn't holding Brian, just sitting confidently by his side. She didn't have any weapon that I could see. I speed-dialed Nate and left my phone open in my pocket. I then came up behind her and put her in a chokehold, yelling, "Run, Brian! Now! Run." He did.

She instantly stood up and pulled me off of my feet for just a second before I touched down again. I held on as she grabbed for her throat. Tightening my grip, I jerked as hard as I could. Sirens blared nearby. She reached into her pocket, pulled out a knife, and sliced my forearm. I let go of her, and suddenly we faced each other, just as we had at the gym with the weight bench between us. Was our deadly confrontation inevitable? Every time I chose to avoid it, I was driven back to this standoff.

Onlookers moved back, and some began to scatter in panic. Brian hid behind the fountain, but I could see that he wasn't leaving the area. It made me like him even more to think that he cared enough to stay, but I wished he had kept running.

Squads pulled up into the small parking lot behind us. Camille looked over her shoulder toward them before reaching into her pocket. I didn't wait to see what she retrieved. Diving behind a garbage can, I heard a shot. Camille took off in a sprint, heading straight for Brian. I got up to head her off, but I was worried about giving her an easy target. I felt a vague pain in my arm and warm blood flowing onto my hand.

When Brian saw her coming, he ran across the road. She saw him, but veered away, choosing the Lake Walk as her escape route. He was no longer in danger. I called to him. He turned, and seeing only me, stopped. He ran back as fast as he could and slammed into me. We both nearly toppled over, but I grabbed and held onto him with my good arm. My right arm was bleeding quite heavily, so I said, "Hang on, buddy, I've got to do something here."

"You're hurt," he said.

"It doesn't really hurt, it just looks bad," I said, trying to reassure him. "Can I borrow your shirt?" He shrugged out of it in an instant. It was a little grubby, but it would stop the bleeding. I pulled it around my arm, and he tied it for me quite adeptly.

Once that was done, I held my arm up in the air. Police officers ran past us in pursuit of Camille. I thought I saw Nate run by, too. Brian and I worked our way back over to the fountain and sat down.

"You okay?" He looked at my arm, then at me.

I grinned at him. "You really are a great kid, aren't you? I'm fine. Nothing a few stitches won't take care of."

He put his head in his hands and moaned. "That was fucking scary!"

I laughed and nodded in agreement. "How'd she get you?"

"She came to my school and said she was a probation officer. They pulled me from class, and she took me outside. When we were both out of sight of the teachers, she grabbed me and tossed me into a car. I thought, 'Man, who is this PO, and what the hell did I do?' It wasn't a squad car, though, and she put me in the front."

For some reason, his familiarity with being picked up by the police hit my funny bone, and I could feel a fit of hysterical laughter rising in my throat. I actually started to giggle. He looked at me with concern. "Then she said she'd kill you if I didn't cooperate."

That sobered me up.

"I didn't argue with her. She is one large, tough woman. I can't believe you took her on."

"I can't either, really. Good thing I didn't have too much time to think about it." My arm was starting to throb, but I tried not to show it. Nate came running back to check on us, and I stood up to greet him.

"I have to get to the hospital." I gestured with my bloody arm.

"I'll take you," he said.

"Did you get her?" I had to know.

"Not yet, but we're working on it."

Up ahead, I saw Camille's car pulling out of a lot. "That's her, in the Forester," I said, pointing with my good arm. Either the police were idiots, or she was just lucky. In any case, she was getting away again. Nate looked at me for permission.

"Go! The hospital is three blocks from here. We'll walk."

He bolted for his car while yelling into his portable radio. The chase was on again. I had zero confidence that they would catch her. I was beginning to believe the entire Duluth Police Department couldn't catch her.

Brian stayed with me until I was stitched up. I called Karen at the Probation Office, and she came to take him home. I knew Karen would have a hard time explaining all of this to Brian's mom, but what other option did we have? I didn't want him to be held in detention for something that wasn't his fault.

"Make sure your mom locks the house tonight," I told him, as he left the hospital with a wave. They had given him scrubs to wear home since his shirt was ruined.

All told, I had thirty stitches. I didn't think I could drive my cycle home, so I called Zoey.

I walked back down to the Rose Garden to wait. Taking in the emerging flower beds, the beauty of the lake, and the people enjoying an ordinary spring day, I couldn't comprehend how different it had felt only a little while earlier.

When Zoey arrived, we sat on the fountain bench for a few minutes while I told her about Camille's latest escape. She didn't seem angry. She simply got up, asked me for the motorcycle keys, and said she'd take it home. She tossed me her keys and walked off. I watched her put my helmet on, fire up the bike, and ride off like it was routine. Like me being knifed was routine.

I drove with my arm up for the entire half-hour commute. Zoey was nowhere in sight. I could feel each pulse in my arm, but I welcomed the distraction. I was really worried about what was going on with Zoey. When I pulled up in front of Kathy and Donna's house, Zoey was sitting on the porch waiting for me. I approached gently. She had an apologetic smile on her face.

"I'm sorry, babe," she said.

I just raised my eyebrows. "No, I'm the one who's sorry."

"No, I shouldn't have left you like that. You're hurt, and I stormed off before thinking. Halfway home, I wondered. 'Shit, can she even drive with that arm?' I was caught up in me. I'm just so afraid of losing you. All the time. I mean it's every day. Something has happened every day. Big things, you know?" She put her head in her hands, much like Brian had done. I sat beside her.

"We've been through too much. We both need this to end."

"You need a gun," she said.

"I don't want a gun."

"What if she had pulled a gun on you today rather than a knife?" She looked me in the eyes.

"She did pull a gun on me."

Zoey moaned and shook her head.

I didn't have a response. I didn't want to live my life this way, either. I tried to explain. "It was about Brian. I couldn't live with myself if she'd hurt him because of me."

"I'm sure he's a great kid," she said.

"He is. In spite of where he comes from. I mean, he has a skinhead, hate-mongering, paranoid father; crooks for brothers; and a doormat for a mom. Yet he has a heart of gold. Sure, he's stumbled and made mistakes, but the right PO could make all the difference for him. It doesn't take that much to help these kids."

"Hon, I love that you have a passion for helping young people. I just wish it didn't involve getting you hurt or killed." She looked at my bandaged arm.

I felt the guilt start eating away at me again, but I made a conscious decision to silence the voice of self-doubt in my head. "Do you realize, Zoey, that this whole stalking ordeal had nothing to do with my work?" The possibility that Camille had been behind this whole thing from the start and that the Jones connection wasn't really a connection at all was becoming obvious. Maybe my job hadn't been the cause of any of the chasing or the voyeurism.

She contemplated the question for a moment before say, "You may be right about that."

"I have some other bad news for you," I said.

Her mouth dropped open. "What else could there possibly be?"

I told Zoey about Camille shooting Randy at our house. That really spooked her.

"Today?"

I nodded. "She probably shot him before coming to find you."

"She's a psychopath," Zoey said without inflection.

I nodded agreement.

"She's just eliminating problems and anyone she perceives to be her enemy."

"Hard to really grasp that," I said.

"Just picture an empty vessel."

"She can get angry and hateful."

"That's all, though. She might be beyond anyone's help."

I just nodded. I had another question for her that I just couldn't get out of my head. It seemed kind of absurd to be focusing on it, but perhaps my mind needed to steer away from the topic of sociopaths.

"Hon?"

Zoey looked at me like I was going to ask another serious question. "What?"

"Where did you learn to ride? I mean, you just hopped on my bike and rode away like it was nothing."

She smiled a little. "I did some dirt bike riding as a kid in Arizona. After playing around in the desert, street bikes are a piece of cake."

I took comfort in the picture that formed in my mind of us riding around Lake Superior together. If Camille could be stopped.

Chapter 33

ZOEY AND I SPENT A GOOD CHUNK of the evening talking in Kathy and Donna's porch with our dogs snuggled up beside us. I told her how she was the most important thing to me no matter what happened with anything else. Before bed, I also sat down with Kathy and thanked her for offering me another job to fall back on. Not a lot of people had that kind of opportunity waiting in the wings.

No one in the house slept well that night, fearing that Camille would somehow invade this happy home more than she already had, but after a quiet weekend, Monday arrived like any ordinary day. Everyone left for work, and Kathy and I puttered around in the shop until lunch. We worked on making raised-panel cabinet door prototypes. I had trouble concentrating because I was waiting for the other shoe to drop.

Part of me wanted to be Zoey's shadow—to stay with her every moment of the day, making sure that Camille wouldn't harm her. If Camille had been thinking symbolically when she cut off Diane's hand, she might decide that depriving me of the love of my life was a fitting revenge.

I felt compelled to draw the threat away from Zoey. I called her to make sure she was okay. Then, instead of going back into the shop, I told Kathy I had to ride. She begged me to stay, but I just took off.

I realized that I didn't have my helmet on. I was too distracted even to do something as routine as put my helmet on. I had to be more careful. Plotting to take on a demented killer, I hadn't even been aware enough to remember ordinary precautions.

My arm throbbed where it had been stitched up, but the pain helped me to focus. From the back of my mind came the belated thought, "You will have scars." I knew the scars from recent events went far beyond the surface of my skin. I had to put a stop to all of it.

The guard assigned to Kathy's house had a look of panic on him as I rode past. I could see him making a phone call to see if he should follow me or stay with the house. When I reached the freeway, I could see him following at a distance. He drove a marked squad, and I found some comfort in the protection.

I didn't know where I was going. It might be safe to go up the north shore, but I wasn't looking for safe. I have a philosophy about what to do when I'm afraid of something. I move toward it. Oddly enough, this had always worked for me. Up until that point, anyway. When something worked, I stuck with it. I found myself pulling into the parking lot of the Rose Garden again. I sat on the same bench Camille had sat on with Brian and pulled out my cell phone. I knew I had her number from when she called me, so I called it. What could it hurt, right? She answered.

"What do you want, bitch?"

"It's Jo. Let's finish this," I said.

"How stupid do you think I am? I'm sure you have a trap set for me."

"I'm sure you are stupid, but there's no trap. Just one cop who's been assigned to protect me."

"Right."

"Whatever. You're blowing your chance."

She was silent.

"How could you kill your own partner?" I felt a need to keep her talking. I had to know what kind of crazy she was.

"My ex-partner, you mean?"

"Diane," I said.

"Because you deserved to go to jail."

"Wasn't this all about Diane in the first place? I mean, weren't you upset because you thought she was with me?"

"She's always been with you. Even when she lived with me. She kept a fucking shrine to you."

"Well, I wasn't with her."

"Don't insult my intelligence."

"Too late for that, I'm afraid," I said in a flat voice. I could hear her breathing. She was angry. There was no way she could resist coming to me. I felt certain she was a psychopath—incapable of feeling anything except about herself, and driven to power.

"Believe me or not, I'm at the Rose Garden." I disconnected.

There was a chance she would refuse to come out of hiding, but I was counting on her to show up. She hated me enough to take the risk. I used a trash barrel to climb on top of the bathroom building so that I could lie down to watch in all directions. The roof eaves were full of dried leaves.

Camille pulled up in her Subaru on London Road a block west of the Rose Garden. She got out of her car and walked toward the lake, presumably to approach from that side. When she got close enough to see that the bench was empty, she fumed. She reached up and fingered something at her waist. A gun? She circled my location. At one point, she looked up. Shit! I was a sitting duck if she saw me. I held my breath and waited. Nothing happened. I slid over a few feet as quietly as I could, and when I peered over the building, she was gone.

I listened closely for foot falls. Hearing none, I shimmied up so that I could get a look around. She was over by my cycle. *No, not my bike! Why did I have to get the same damned kind? Would she know it was mine?* My bodyguard noticed her and keyed his mike. The chase was on again. He waited in his squad, for backup I assumed. I saw Nate pull into the lot. No one was at her car. She saw his unmarked and bolted in the direction from where she had come.

I quickly got down off the building and ran to my cycle. Camille squealed the tires on the little wagon as she fled east. Two squads, Nate's unmarked car, and my Silverwing chased after her.

She took a right on Twenty-first Avenue East and then onto the freeway. The traffic was heavy, and she was tailgating the bumper of a big Buick. The squads engaged their sirens, and most of the traffic pulled over. The gap allowed her to bolt ahead.

The squads were gaining on her and attempting to get into position to block her in, with Nate trailing in his Crown Vic. She sideswiped one of the squads, causing it to hit the side rail and flip over. The second squad stayed with her. She fired a shot, and he swerved and slowed down.

Suddenly I was next to her, unprotected from her fire. I gunned the throttle and raced ahead, swerving quickly to take the on ramp to the Blatnik Bridge. I could see the gun in her hand as she rested it on her steering wheel.

The second squad must have missed the turn. Shit…shit shit shit!! I heard another gunshot.

I accelerated. The Silverwing wasn't built for speed, but I managed to climb up to 85 mph, maneuvering in between cars, trying to put a little distance between us.

There was work being done on the bridge, and the orange cones made me flash on my dream—the dream I had just before firing up my bike for the season. I slowed to avoid a couple of cones and merged into the single lane of traffic that was backed up for half a mile. I skidded to avoid slamming into the car in front of me, feeling exposed like I was a target in a crazy arcade. I turned my head and saw Camille's Subaru weaving in and out of the cones the way I had. Passing the two cars that separated us, she was forced to stop as well.

I jumped off my bike as she climbed out of her car with a gun in her hand. Police sirens screamed from both directions, but blocked by traffic, they might as well have been miles away. It was me against Camille and her gun.

She seemed calm and cold as she exited her vehicle, intent on ending my life. I ran behind a construction vehicle and looked around for a weapon. I wasn't going down without a fight. Reaching down for a piece of rebar, I felt the cold steel of her gun against my head.

My first thought was of Zoey. I instinctively jerked away from the gun and swung my fist around, making contact with her arm. The gun went off like a cannon in my head, but the bullet missed me, and I was still moving. I charged her by ramming my head into her midsection. Camille's gun went flying over the edge. I slowed my own momentum toward the rail by collapsing to my knees. I remember hitting my head on the concrete railing before Camille grabbed me by the throat and shoved me against it. She was lifting me to send me up and over the side when we both heard a familiar voice scream, "STOP!"

Zoey had appeared out of nowhere, riding my black Honda Silverwing. In one fluid motion, she jumped off the cycle and let the force of gravity lay it down on the pavement, where it spun to a halt. While Nate had been impeded by the vehicles between us, Zoey had ridden around the jam of cars until she could get to me. She pointed her handgun at Camille. "You will let her go." Zoey looked like she meant business.

"You're wrong about that," Camille said, a glint of madness shining through her murderous eyes. She lifted me higher, until I was precariously balanced at the edge of a long drop down into the waters of Lake Superior.

I yelled, "No, don't do this. It won't change anything." I meant the message for Zoey as well as for Camille.

Zoey avoided looking at me. Instead, those penetrating green eyes studied Camille. Then Zoey very deliberately tossed her gun over the side of the bridge.

Well, at least my girl was coming to her senses about guns, but I wasn't sure this would end well.

"You can't win, Camille. What good will any of this do?" Zoey asked. She had a way of drawing secrets from people with her questions, even when they didn't think they knew the answers.

"Diane never loved me. And it's Jo's fault." Her grip tightened on my neck, and I struggled to breathe.

"Why did Diane live with you if she didn't love you? She must have had some feelings for you."

I was glad that Zoey was trying to help Camille without resorting to gunfire, but first I wished she could convince her to let me down off that railing.

"All she could think about was Jo, Jo, Jo. I'm going to make sure no one ever loves Jo again."

"You can't make sure of that. I will always love Jo."

Camille turned her crazed eyes toward Zoey. Sad, empty eyes. Camille couldn't seem to comprehend the words she was hearing. Her hold on my throat tightened.

Gulls screamed overhead as they swooped in midair. I thought I might soon join them in a diving final flight of my own. Then everything went black.

Chapter 34

I WOKE UP IN A HOSPITAL BED with Zoey holding my hand. When I opened my eyes, she kissed me, whispering, "You shithead."

I had the worst headache of my life, but I couldn't help laughing. "Nice to see you, too."

She shook her head at me and climbed up next to me in the bed. "No more, okay? No more."

"What happened?" I vaguely recalled a chase on the bridge and Zoey arriving with her gun.

"You need to let the memory come back to you on your own. But I can tell you that psychopaths can be reasoned with."

"You stopped Camille?"

"She's in custody. You're safe." She stroked my face.

I tried to sit up, but my head hurt like crazy. "I hit my head on the concrete rail."

She nodded. "That's what caused your concussion."

I felt dizzy and gave in to sleep.

When I woke up next, Kathy and Donna were there along with Nate.

The first words out of his mouth were, "Stupid shit."

My head still hurt. He went on to tell me that the police had matched the slug that had killed Randy to Camille's gun. Once I was stable, Zoey described how she had talked Camille into letting me live after I lost consciousness.

"She seemed to be fascinated by how much I resembled Diane, and so she listened. I told her that she could be a different person, a person someone could truly love. Her ego was fragile. She had experienced so much rejection and abandonment that simply acknowledging that she had the potential to

177

love and be loved got through to her."

"Apparently, the thrill of killing me lost some of its appeal when I was out cold. How did you know where to find me?"

"That was a fluke," she said. "I wanted to surprise you, so I went to pick up your bike, which was no longer needed in Diane's murder investigation. The guys at the impound lot were listening to a police scanner and were all excited about a high-speed chase heading for the Blatnik Bridge. They mentioned Camille's name, and I knew you might be in trouble."

The doctors kept me for observation for another day before releasing me.

Zoey had cleaned up our house and had even done some kind of ritual with sage before bringing me home from the hospital.

Then she asked me what my plans were. I told her that I needed to see what happened with my ethics review committee. She wouldn't let me get away with that and asked, "But what is it that *you* want to do?"

"I need to work with kids, Zoey. It's who I am. Maybe I could find a career helping kids in another way, but this is my calling. A hundred more Brians are waiting for me out there. They need competent and caring probation officers. I can't let them down."

She struggled with wanting me to pick another career that was less dangerous but let me work with kids. I vacillated, too. It also pissed me off that the ethics review board was even reviewing this. I had been cleared of all charges in Diane's murder. While I had not worked within the DPD's plan in tracking down Camille, I hadn't broken any laws.

After a couple days of walking the dogs, puttering around my shop, and waiting to hear about the review, I called Nate. He came out. Over coffee and cookies, I asked him about Camille. He said she might qualify for commitment as criminally insane, but that those patients rarely ever see the light of freedom once they're locked up. He assured me that Zoey and I wouldn't have to worry about her again.

I called my boss and asked permission to visit Brian. I wanted to buy him a new shirt to replace the one he had sacrificed to stop the bleeding on my arm after Camille cut me. The Chief allowed me to go, as long as Brian's mother was home.

I had learned from Nate that Brian's father and his older brothers had been arrested and were going away for a long time. Nate had successfully tied them to the arsons, and no judge in his or her right mind was going to let them out before trial. I called Brian's mom and made plans to meet at their home on Friday after school.

I asked Zoey to accompany me. I needed her to understand firsthand what the pull of my work really was. She didn't question my motives. As we stopped in front of the house, I gave her hand a quick squeeze. She smiled at me, and we walked up the short sidewalk together. Brian's mom came to the door and asked us in. I held out the package I had brought Brian. "Would you like me to leave this with you, or should I give it to Brian?"

"Please come in. You can give it to him yourself. He'll be very happy to see you." She yelled up the stairs, "Brian, honey, someone's here to see you."

I heard movement upstairs, and Brian came running down. His enthusiasm was barely contained, but he tried to look cool. "Hey, Jo." He smiled.

His mom looked at him sharply. "Ms. Spence, Brian."

"Mom, she said I could call her Jo."

Mrs. Jones put her hand on his shoulder. "Okay."

"I wanted to thank you," I said, "for helping me get to the hospital the other day. You were very brave." He stood a little taller.

"No problem." He shrugged.

"I got you a shirt to replace the one we wrecked."

"Cool! Thanks," he said, as he looked in the package at the brightly colored material. "Hey, you got a bunch of them."

Leading us into the kitchen, Brian's mother offered us coffee. I was beginning to like her a lot. She updated us on the status of her other boys and husband before asking if I had anything to do with the fact that Brian hadn't been arrested. I shook my head, wondering the same thing. Brian spoke up.

"She sure did, mom. I was at my PO's office or in group when some of the shit, er...aah, sorry, stuff went down. If Jo hadn't tried to help me, I would have been right there with them."

I smiled at him. "That means you got yourself out of trouble, Brian. You made the choice to stay away from your brothers and do the right thing."

"Never would have seen probation as a good thing before you, though."

"I'm sure you would have. You're a good kid who was caught up in a bad situation. Things will be easier as time goes on."

"Well, whatever the cause, I thank you both," Mrs. Jones said. "At least I still have him." She smiled at Brian. He gave her an embarrassed smile back, blushing. "Things are better already, aren't they, Brian?"

He nodded. "I'm not smoking pot anymore, and I'm going to school every day."

"Excellent!" I said.

On our way back to the car, I spotted a tall blond woman walking away from us. Just as she turned the corner at the end of the block, I grabbed Zoey's arm. "Did you see that?"

She looked at me. "What?"

I shook my head, afraid to say it out loud. "I thought I saw Camille."

Zoey looked more closely at me.

"It's okay, hon. She's locked away now. Let's drive by so you can see for yourself."

We drove around the block. The only person we saw was a man walking a tiny dog. I wondered if I would continue to see Camille everywhere.

On the drive home, Zoey turned to me.

"I get why you love your job."

I nodded. "Our problems may not have been about my job at all. Do you see why I can't give up such a core part of who I am?"

"Can you work with kids in a different way?"

"This is it for me. It's what I do. It's what I used to do, anyway. I'm not clear of the ethics board yet."

She reached for my hand. "We'll cross that bridge together. And you're right. I can't ask you to give up who you are. I love that person way too much." She was still with me.

The ethics review came about a week later. My boss and the chief were there, but the committee was made up of administrators from various county offices and a couple of commissioners. My union lawyer sat beside me, and Zoey, Kathy, and Donna were among the group of friends occupying the spectator seats in the large courtroom.

One of the commissioners began the review by summarizing the bad press and damage to the image of the Probation Office that had occurred because of my personal problems. My lawyer objected, saying that all charges had been cleared and that this entire inquiry was revictimizing the real victim in all of this.

I sat silently as each party weighed in. Most of the county managers found no grounds for an inquiry and gave their view that any negative publicity could be righted if the agency put out public statements highlighting my heroism. One of the commissioners mentioned my lifestyle as a concern. My lawyer pressed him to articulate his statement more clearly. He had enough sense to keep his thoughts to himself. The County Attorney waited for a lull in the proceedings before clearing her throat.

"Clearly, no laws have been broken here. No violations of the ethics code have been identified. If this committee renders a finding of violation, I can guarantee you the county will in all likelihood face and lose a lawsuit for discrimination. A very costly lawsuit, and neither I nor any member of my staff will have a leg to stand on in court. My recommendation to you is to close this inquiry for lack of basis." She continued to stand and leveled a look at the two commissioners that could freeze fire.

I knew at that instant that if I were male and not a lesbian, the inquiry would never have taken place. I looked at Zoey, and our eyes locked in a promise to fight this thing to the living end, should it take that turn. They ended discussion and attempted to make a closed vote. My attorney challenged them to be transparent in their process. It was all being recorded anyway and subject to public record. She cautioned that secrecy could and certainly would be interpreted poorly. The vote was nine to two in favor of dismissing the inquiry for lack of cause.

Kathy, Donna, Zoey, and I went out to brunch at the Roost, a rooftop restaurant one block from the courthouse that rotates 360 degrees per hour, giving diners a spectacular view of Duluth's harbor, downtown, and hillside. While my friends were disappointed in my decision to return to work, we all high-fived the victory, sipped gourmet brew, and consumed a gigantic buffet breakfast.

On our way out of the restaurant, I spotted a black Subaru wagon parked a block away. I wondered to myself if I didn't have some kind of

PTSD from being chased for so long, and so determinedly. This was a black wagon. Camille's green one had been impounded by the police.

I still had lingering aches and pains in my neck from my collision with the bridge guardrail. As I massaged my neck, Zoey looked over at me.

"Still sore?"

"Nothing a good back rub won't cure."

She rolled her eyes a tad and then followed my stare—at a tall, short-haired blond woman exiting the Subaru. I tensed.

"Can't be her," Zoey said.

"I know that in here." I pointed to my head. "But my heart needs some time and some healing." I wanted to believe that Camille was securely institutionalized, but part of me needed more time to trust that we were really safe.

Zoey said, "That's true. We both need to be patient with ourselves."

I took her hand as we strolled along the city street, feeling our connection and the sweet feeling of not being stalked anymore.

"Don't look now," Zoey added, "but it seems Mack is really enjoying your Range Rover." She nodded toward my former vehicle parked at an odd angle across from us. I could see something that looked like a full moon shining out the driver's side window. "You really need to get him in for some treatment."

Acknowledgments

CHARLENE BROWN. You are a rock star editor and publisher. Thank you so much for your patience, skill, and support. There are many better writers out there who are unpublished. Without you, I would be one of them. I'm so lucky to have you in my life.

TO MY CLOVER VALLEY FRIENDS who always read early drafts: Karen Andrews, Judith Torrence, Gail Polesak, Mary Anne Daniel. You encouraged me to go with my strengths. Thank you for your support and input.

TO MY SHARP AND DEDICATED PROOFREADERS: Char Appelwick and Dave Heath. Thanks for investing your time in this project.

KARI. I can't remember a single time you were cranky about my writing. I think it's because you know it makes me so happy. It could also be that it's the only time I sit still when the TV is off. Whatever the reason, thank you for your encouragement and love.

FANS. For those fans who take the time to email me that you enjoyed the book or that it had an impact on you, thank you. It keeps me writing.

beingjenwright@gmail.com

About the Author

JEN WRIGHT LIVES, loves, works, plays, and writes in Duluth, Minnesota, and in the small community of Clover Valley. She is an avid hiker and cross-country skier, and she finds writing of any kind relaxing and entertaining. Her partner Kari is funny, kind, and doesn't really like the outdoor lifestyle they share, or living in the country, for that matter...except for hanging out on their deck. They share a love for their dogs, Kari's grandkids, and camping in their Toyota motor home. In Jen's real-life job, she works as a Probation Supervisor.

Clover Valley Press specializes in producing quality books written by women of the northland.

For author guidelines or to purchase copies of our books, go to www.clovervalleypress.com.

CLOVER
VALLEY
PRESS

www.ingramcontent.com/pod-product-compliance
Lightning Source LLC
Chambersburg PA
CBHW060058260626
47160CB00005B/1708